THE GREAT WAR HAS BEGUN AND POOR
HICCUP HORRENDOUS HADDOCK
THE THIRD IS AN OUTCAST. AFRAID AND
ALONE, HE'S IN A TERRIBLE MESS, WHEN
ALL HE WAS TRYING TO DO WAS SAVE THE
DRAGONS FROM EXTINCTION.

Now Hiccup's the Enemy of the Wilderwest
(and rather smelly) and the rampant **DRAGON
FURIOUS** *really* wants to kill him. Meanwhile,
Hiccup really wants to rescue his captured father
Stoick the Vast and find his lost friend Fishlegs
– oh and the precious Dragon Jewel, which
could be **ANYWHERE**.

Can Hiccup the Outcast succeed in his Quest
and become **HICCUP THE HERO** once again?

You don't **HAVE** to read the Hiccup books in order.
But if you want to, this is the right order:

1. How to train your Dragon
2. How to be a Pirate
3. How to speak Dragonese
4. How to Cheat a Dragon's Curse
5. How to Twist a Dragon's Tale
6. A Hero's Guide to Deadly Dragons
7. How to Ride a Dragon's Storm
8. How to Break a Dragon's Heart
9. How to Steal a Dragon's Sword
10. How to Seize a Dragon's Jewel
11. How to Betray a Dragon's Hero
12. How to Fight a Dragon's Fury

JOIN HICCUP ON HIS QUEST
(although he doesn't quite realise he is on one yet...)

THE PROPHECY OF
THE KING'S LOST THINGS

'The Dragontime is coming
And only a King can save you now.
The King shall be the
Champion of Champions.

You shall know the King
By the King's Lost Things.
A fang-free dragon, my second-best sword,
My Roman shield,
An arrow-from-the-land-that-does-not-exist,
The heart's stone, the key-that-opens-all-locks,
The ticking-thing, the Throne, the Crown.

And last and best of all the ten,
The Dragon Jewel shall save all men.'

HICCUP
(the
Hero of
this
story)

Wodensfang
(Hiccup's hunting dragon)

Eggingarde

TOOTHLESS
(Hiccup's hunting-dragon)

STOICK the VAST
(Hiccup's father)

That delightful villain ALVIN the Treacherous (now King-in-Waiting to the Wilderwest)

the Wicked witch Excellinor (Alvin's mother)

WINDWALKER (Hiccup's riding dragon)

This book is dedicated to Xanny Cowell

HODDER CHILDREN'S BOOKS

First published in Great Britain in 2012 by Hodder & Stoughton
This edition published in 2017 by Hodder & Stoughton

16

Text and illustrations copyright © 2012 Cressida Cowell

The moral rights of the author have been asserted.

A CIP catalogue record for this book is available from the British Library.

ISBN: 978 1 444 90879 4

Cover design by Jennifer Stephenson
Background cover illustration by Christopher Gibbs

"The Neverland is a map of a boy's mind..." J. M. Barrie 'Peter Pan'

Printed and bound by CPI Group (UK) Ltd, Croydon, CR0 4YY

The paper and board used in this book are made from wood from responsible sources.

MIX
Paper from
responsible sources
FSC® C104740

Hodder Children's Books
An imprint of Hachette Children's Group, Part of Hodder & Stoughton
Carmelite House, 50 Victoria Embankment, London EC4Y 0DZ
An Hachette UK Company
www.hachette.co.uk

THANK YOU
to Anne McNeil, Naomi Pottesman,
Jennifer Stephenson, Judit Konar,
and most importantly, Simon Cowell

How to Seize a
Dragon's Jewel

written and illustrated by
CRESSIDA COWELL

Hodder
Children's
Books

Hiccup Horrendous
Haddock the Third

~ CONTENTS ~

PROLOGUE BY HICCUP HORRENDOUS HADDOCK III

Courage.

You, dear reader, will need courage to read on.

This is NOT the last of my memoirs. But the story has become darker now, so dark that I need all my courage just to write it.

I am looking back to that time when I was fourteen years old and an Outcast.

The Red-Rage had taken over all the dragons in the land and the Dragon Rebellion had begun. The Great War between humans and dragons had started.

The Vikings were being led by that dreadful villain, Alvin the Treacherous, guided by his even-more-dreadful mother, the Witch Excellinor.

The Dragon Furious was in charge of the dragon forces, and his aim was nothing less than the extinction of the entire Viking race.

And the Dragon Furious was winning.

The Vikings' only hope was for a new King to be crowned King of the Wilderwest. A King who, according to ancient prophecy, would have all ten of the King's Lost Things.

Nine of the Lost Things had been found. Only the Dragon Jewel, the most important, remained Lost.

The Dragon Jewel had the power to destroy dragons for ever... it was the only thing the Dragon Furious was afraid of.

Alvin the Treacherous had eight of the Lost Things.

I, Hiccup the Outcast, had only one: my little hunting-dragon called Toothless. But I also had Grimbeard the Ghastly's map that showed the way to where the Jewel was hidden.

And so I, 'Enemy Traitor Number One', was being hunted through the Archipelago, by both humans and dragons alike. A proclamation calling for my death hung on hundreds of burnt-out tree trunks.

My fourteen-year-old self was all alone apart from three dragon companions.

My Tribe had been driven out of their home on Berk by the Dragon Rebellion.

My father Stoick and my friend Fishlegs had been turned into slaves and sent to the Amber Slavelands. (Originally, they were in the Uglithing Slavelands, but when the witch figured out where

the Jewel was, she moved
everyone.)

You see why I call these
my darkest times?

I had to have hope
that things would turn out
well in the end, that
the small things and the
happiness of peacetime would return.

I had to remember this through the teeth and fire
and talons.

I had to have *Courage*.

WANTED

HICCUP HORRENDOUS HADDOCK III
THE OUTCAST

Kill him on sight.

(His hunting-dragon should be captured alive. HE is needed for the service of the kingdom.)

Alvin the Treacherous

Excellinor the Witch

1. THE WARRIOR

One cold moonlit winter night in the Forgotten Forest, a gigantic Warrior sat high and still in a treetop, like an Angel of Death.

The Warrior was out hunting. It had been on the trail of the Outcast for many days. It was intending to kill this Outcast, this enemy of the Wilderwest.

Its metal visor was down. Its sword was ready in its hand, looking for the kill. It was still as a statue, only its bright blue eyes looking down on the path winding through the woods far below it.

In those times, the humans and the dragons were at war, so it was strictly forbidden for humans to ride dragons any more.

But surprisingly, this Warrior was seated on the back of a dragon, lying lazy but alert along the length of the tree branch. The dragon was an Air Dragon of the purest silver; very, very rare and very, very dangerous.

It too looked down at the snowy path below, only its pointed tail moving, slowly and rhythmically, like the tail of a cat.

All was quiet. After a little time, a noise was heard. The Warrior had closed its eyes, but now, buried in the black visor, they snapped open.

Way in the distance, a human was
moving along the path through the woods.

The human was 'The Outcast', the Enemy,
exactly the person that the Warrior was waiting
to kill.

The Warrior gave a grunt of satisfaction, and sat up a little straighter.

When you looked at this Outcast close-up (which the Warrior couldn't, not from that distance) he was not at all what you might imagine an Outcast to be. He was very different from the clever confident figure he cut when he was releasing dragons from right under the Visithugs' noses two hours ago.

He was a young boy called Hiccup Horrendous Haddock the Third, about fourteen years old, very skinny and ordinary-looking, with the dark purple mark that the humans called the 'Slavemark' – a tattoo in the shape of a dragon – burning blue-black on one side of his forehead.

Hiccup had been sleeping rough for a year now, in treetops, or in caves, and all he'd had to eat in that time was berries and nuts and food stolen fearfully from sleeping Viking villages.

Risking his life day after day undoing the dragon-traps the Vikings had been setting for the dragons, and constantly running away from the humans *and* the terrifying hunting-dragons of the Dragon Rebellion had really taken it out of him.

So there in the moonlight, Hiccup looked like what he was.

Afraid, alone.

He was dressed from head to toe in a dragonskin fire-suit, ripped and tattered by brambles and branches. He was muddy and dirty, the strain and fear of being hunted showing in the stiffness of his body, and the anxious tic in his eyes.

He had a black eye, and he was limping, as was the riding-dragon trotting along beside him. The Windwalker was exhausted, which was why Hiccup wasn't riding him, and puffing out great wafts of tired steam.

Around Hiccup's head fluttered two tiny hunting-dragons. One very old one, the Wodensfang, with wings all tattered and torn. One very young one, Toothless, a bright grass-green – the naughtiest, most fidgety dragon in the whole of the Archipelago.

They were talking together in soft whispers in Dragonese.

your Quest is very simple

'I'm telling you, Hiccup,' the
Wodensfang was saying in a light
quavery voice, 'your Quest is very simple.

'You have to find the Dragon Jewel, go
to Tomorrow, get yourself crowned King of the
Wilderwest, and then the Tomorrow Men will tell
you the secret of the Dragon Jewel and you can stop
this stupid war, and save the dragons and the
humans from extinction.'

'Did you s-s-see me?' squeaked Toothless. 'Did
you see me dive-bombing that Visithug? Wasn't I
clever? Wasn't I brilliant? Wasn't I m-marvellous?'

Did You see me dive-bombing that Visithug?

'Yes, you were marvellous, Toothless,' replied Hiccup, 'but can you keep it down a bit. The forest dragons are hibernating at the moment, and we don't want to wake them up.'

He rubbed the back of his neck, and sighed, because he was missing everybody so much. Being an Outcast was very, very lonely.

'The thing is, Wodensfang, nothing is ever that simple. People actually have to want me, a slave, an Outcast, to be King. You have to have actual human followers, not just you three. And I have to have all of the Lost Things, and Alvin the Treacherous already has eight of them.'

'You've got m-m-me!' squeaked Toothless, landing on Hiccup's arm. '*I'm* one of the Lost Things, and I'm the best one!'

'*Manners*,' reminded the Windwalker gently. 'Don't forget, Toothless, no boasting...'

'OK,' said Toothless, his brow furrowing. 'Toothless is the best one... p-p-please?'

'The map says that the Jewel is in the Amber Slavelands,' said the Wodensfang. 'Why aren't we there?'

26

'Because instinctively I don't think the Jewel is there,' replied Hiccup.

'That is because your heart is not yet in your Quest,' replied the Wodensfang, solemnly. 'At the moment, you are on a different Quest, the Quest to find your friend Fishlegs and your father. Admit it, that's why we're here.'

It *was* why they were there. The Hooligans were supposed to have hidden out in this country after Berk was burnt out by the Dragon Furious.

'OK,' admitted Hiccup. 'I am worried about Fishlegs, he's always sort of relied on me.'

Fishlegs was a 'runt' who had been washed up on the beaches of Berk fourteen years ago. He had no parents, so it was Hiccup who looked after him and stopped the other Hooligans from bullying him.

'And this is getting in the way of your true Quest,' interrupted the Wodensfang, 'which is to find the Dragon Jewel.'

'Not entirely,' said Hiccup, 'because I still don't think the Jewel is in the Amber Slavelands, whatever the map says.'

They had walked such a long way now, that they stopped right underneath the tree the Warrior was sitting in. Hiccup got out the map.

Map to Find the Lost Jewel of GRIMBEARD THE GHASTLY

The Dragontime is Coming
And only a King can save you now
The King shall be the Champion of.
You shall know the King by the Champions
King's Lost Things.

A fang-free dragon, my
second-best sword, my Roman
shield, an arrow-from-the-land-that-
does-not-exist, the heart's stone,
the key-that-opens-all-locks,
the ticking-thing, the Throne,
the Crown.

And last and best of all the ten,
THE DRAGON JEWEL
shall save all men.

The map was quite complicated. It showed a nice distinct picture of the Amber Slavelands, and there was a maze of mirrors and Prison Darkheart, and there, in the heart of it, was the Dragon Jewel, helpfully pointed out with a large arrow and capital letters.

The three dragons peered at it over Hiccup's shoulder. So too did the Warrior and the dragon perched high, invisible and menacing in the treetops above Hiccup.

'Look,' said Hiccup, pointing to a large fish at the top of the map – a fish so long that it took up the entire space from left to right. 'What is that?'

Trust sea-faring creatures like dragons and Vikings to know their fish species.

'It's a member of the herring family,' said the Wodensfang.

'And what colour is it?'

'R-r-red!' said Toothless proudly. 'Ask me another one! I know *all* the colours,' he confided confidentially to the Windwalker.

Toothless knows ALL the colours...

'You see,' said Hiccup, 'in the human world a "red herring" is another way of saying a false start, or a wrong direction. My knowledge of Grimbeard the Ghastly is that he was a tricky man, and this is his way of saying that the Jewel isn't in the Slavelands at all. What do you think, Wodensfang?'

The Wodensfang was the only one of the four of them old enough to have actually met Grimbeard the Ghastly, more than one hundred years before. So now he looked back through time to remember that dreadful man, and what that look told him was that Grimbeard was the trickiest trickster since the great trickster god Loki put his Particularly Tricky Hat on.

'Hmm...' said the Wodensfang. It did seem exactly the sort of thing that Grimbeard would do. And suddenly a maze of mirrors seemed an unlikely thing to be finding in Prison Darkheart, which was probably furnished on the basic side.

Then the Wodensfang raised a cunning eyebrow. 'But it could be a double-bluff...'

'So,' said the soft gentle voice of the raggedy Windwalker, 'if the Dragon Jewel isn't in the Amber Slavelands, where then exactly is it?'

'That's why it's not so simple,' said Hiccup, waving wide his arms. 'It could be anywhere!'

DANGER!!

DANGER!!

At that moment, there was a definite rustle from above, as the hidden Warrior and the hidden dragon craned forward with interest to see what was written on Hiccup's map.

The effect on the four companions below was immediate.

The Wodensfang shot up a foot in the air, its tattered ears turning electrically rigid and purply red and pointing first west, then south, then east, then north.

'Danger!' squeaked the Wodensfang in

the loudest whisper
he could whisper.

'Danger! Quick! Hiccup, get
your helmet on!'

'Oh... no, guys, really...
it's far too big... I find it
easier to fight without it...'

But the dragons
ganged up on him, three
to one.

'You need
it!' whispered
the Wodensfang.
'Remember back on Danger-Brute
Island when you nearly lost
your ear? And that poison dart
that just missed you when you
were undoing the Visithug
dragon-traps?'

'And what about the Head-lopping incident with the Head-loppers over in Nowhere?' The Windwalker padded anxiously back and forward.

'A helmet wouldn't save you from having your head lopped off,' argued Hiccup.

'The Wodensfang is r-r-right!' agreed Toothless, who was agreeing with the Wodensfang more and more these days. Squeaking, the Wodensfang and Toothless lifted the detested helmet from the back of Hiccup's rucksack and with the help of the Windwalker they tenderly jammed it on Hiccup's head.

It was an old Visithug one that they had burgled a couple of weeks ago, and it was a very bad fit.

'It's really uncomfortable,' grumbled Hiccup. 'Plus the big feather thing-y makes me very

The three dragons tenderly jammed the helmet on Hiccup's head memorable. I'm supposed to be undercover you know. An Outcast has to melt into the background...'

'Sssh...' The Wodensfang put his wing to his lips.

'I told you,' said the Wodensfang, 'I've had this really bad feeling that the Dragon Furious has sent some new dragon to assassinate you... Something really terrifying...'

'Yes, Wodensfang,' said Hiccup. 'You're always getting these feelings, but listen, it's all gone quiet.'

'That's the thing about this new dragon, though,' whispered the Wodensfang. 'It's almost undetectable. It's one of those tracker dragons.'

The four companions stretched their ears out into the white muffled world of trees-and-snow.

oing
boing
boing

"Oh no, guys, it's fAr too big..."

Nothing.

'Maybe it was a false alarm,' whispered Toothless.

Up in the treetops the
Warrior and the dragon sat still
as stones. Not a leaf moved,
the forest seemed to hold its
breath...
And then...

RROOOAOOWW

With a scream as loud as a charging baboon, the Warrior hidden in the tree-canopy above exploded into action, erupting from the foliage and descending from above in a shower of leaves and broken branches like some swooping noble nightmare of revenge.

Sssspppppppppppooooooooooow! Zzzzziiiiiiiinggggg!

If Hiccup and the Windwalker hadn't been living on their nerves for the past year, they might not have dodged backward so fast, and Hiccup would have been deader than a dodo.

For the *Zzzzing!* that zinged past Hiccup's nose was the zing of an arrow that missed him by inches and buried itself in a tree trunk a couple of feet behind him.

CLANG! The dodging backwards brought his visor clanging down, where it jammed tight shut.

Uh-oh, thought Hiccup, who was an intelligent boy. *This person wants to kill me.*

BONG! BONG! BONG! Three more arrows came

raining harmlessly off the detestable helmet.

Thanks, guys. The helmet was a good call, thought Hiccup as he jumped onboard the Windwalker, who shot off through the trees.

And then he couldn't believe his eyes when he looked over his shoulder and saw the dragon that was following them.

Oh for Thor's sake.

You couldn't mistake that particular dragon.

It was the Silver Phantom.

Even though it was the dead of night, every silver scale was lit up and shone brighter than was strictly possible in real life. The Silver Phantom seemed to give off its own light, like the moon. Its scream was so high and so loud that it felt as if it was setting fire to your ears.

And as it screamed it poured out a jet of bright blue flame that blasted the trees in front of it, burning their leaves as bright as green stars before dropping to the ground in powdery black smithereens.

The Silver Phantom was absolutely unmistakable.

It was unique.

It also just so happened to be the riding-dragon that belonged to Hiccup's mother.

Which meant that the Warrior currently
re-loading her Northbow and taking careful aim at
Hiccup while guiding the screaming Phantom by the
strength of her Warrior knees alone – *that* particular
Warrior, was in fact…

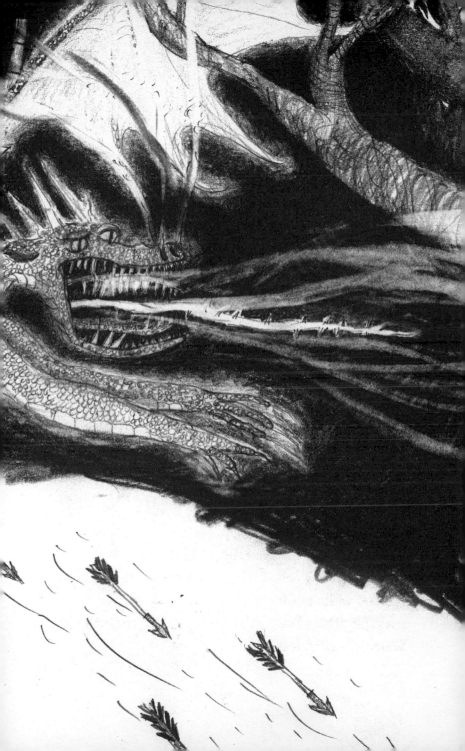

... Hiccup's own mother
Valhallarama.

Silver Phantoms

~ STATISTICS ~

FEAR FACTOR: 10
ATTACK: 10
SPEED: 10
SIZE: 10
DISOBEDIENCE: 10

Some of the Air Dragons fly at such high altitudes that humans have never even seen them. A Silver Phantom is one such dragon: glimpsed very rarely at astonishingly high distances, these sorts of dragons are sometimes known as 'ghosts' and some people doubt they exist at all.

2. A FEW LITTLE COMMUNICATION PROBLEMS

'STOP! MOTHER! IT'S ME, HICCUP!' shouted Hiccup.

But of course the visor on the beastly helmet was down, and so it came out more like: 'Mff! Mff! Mff!'

Hiccup grabbed at the visor and tried to yank it up, but it was jammed absolutely tight shut. It would not budge.

Oh for Thor's sake.

This was not a good situation. Apart from anything else, Valhallarama was a truly magnificent Hero, one of the very, very best, so they were in big trouble if he couldn't tell her who he was.

The thing was, Valhallarama was away questing a lot.

Hiccup was never quite sure what she was questing *for* exactly, but his father, Stoick the Vast, always assured him it was very important.

As a result Hiccup hadn't seen her in a very long while, perhaps for as long as two years now. So she very well might not be aware that her only son was the one who was now known as the Outcast and the Enemy of the Wilderwest. Let alone that Stoick was now a slave, and Hiccup had the Slavemark himself, and a whole load of other things Hiccup was hoping to explain to her gently in a quiet moment.

He had hoped that if he ever did get a chance to explain the whole thing to her, about how what he was really trying to do was save all the dragons from extinction, she might be one of the few people who would actually be on his side. (Hiccup had a hopeful nature.)

Because Valhallarama loved dragons.

Hiccup knew she loved dragons.

At least, he *thought* he knew she loved dragons.

It suddenly occurred to Hiccup, in that moment as they were screaming through the forest at breakneck speed in the dead of night with his mother shooting arrows at him almost continuously, that perhaps he did not really know his mother all that well.

She had been away questing *a lot*.

The Wodensfang and Toothless were both exceptionally speedy so they were flying not at their top speed but on either side of Hiccup's head, like twin dragonly guardian angels.

'You have to admit he is a marvellous Warrior,' quavered the Wodensfang admiringly.

'How big do you think he is? Six foot three? Six foot four? I don't think I've seen a better Warrior since Squidshanks the Frightening... It was a bit before your time, maybe six hundred years ago...'

'She's a *she*! Not a he!' Hiccup shouted back.

But through the helmet it just sounded like 'Mff! Mff! Mff!'

We've all been in this situation. Well, maybe not *precisely* in this situation. But we all know what it's like to have something important to say to a loved one, but something seems to be getting in the way.

The truth is, it is often difficult to explain things to a parent. And most definitely it is particularly difficult when your mother is hunting you at top speed through a dark forest under the impression that you are the Enemy of the Wilderwest.

The Windwalker had grown into an exceptionally fast dragon, and it was smaller than the Phantom, so its more manoeuvrable size meant it could just about keep ahead, flicking through the maze of trees.

MF

mff...
mff...

But still the Phantom was gaining.
'He's going to catch us if we stay
down here,' said Toothless. 'Why d-d-
don't we go up?'

Over the past year
they had often eluded dragon
pursuers by climbing up into
the higher air, too high for other
dragons to follow. Most dragons prefer
shallow air, the air nearest the ground. Very few can
operate in the higher atmosphere.

Apart from the
Silver Phantom.

Hiccup wanted to tell them
that this would be pointless. The
Phantom was an Air Dragon. They
were among the best flyers in the
dragon world, and they flew the
fastest and the highest.

Valhallarama had trained herself not to pass out.
But of course he couldn't tell them that because of the
jammed helmet.

The Windwalker slightly mistimed a slalom,
swayed crazily, and the pursuing Phantom caught him
by the leg, but didn't quite get a good hold, so the
Windwalker wriggled desperately out of the grip and
shot upwards in a blind panic.

'Oh no...' breathed Hiccup, desperately trying to
get him to fly downwards again, but the Windwalker
was crazed with fear and panicking madly, so he just
climbed up and up and up.

Hiccup looked down. The forest was already a dark smudge beneath them.

And out of that smudge burst the Silver Phantom, shooting upwards in a glorious silver arc.

Up, up, it soared with two mighty swoops of its silver wings. It was way too fast for the poor Windwalker, and leapt o-o-o-over their heads in an athletic silver leap, and as it leapt, Valhallarama leant over and plucked Hiccup from the Windwalker's back with her left arm.

Down swooped the Phantom, with Hiccup swinging from his mother's arm, back through the canopy of trees, landing on the forest floor.

Still holding Hiccup by the scruff of his waistcoat, she bounded from the Phantom's back, leant Hiccup against a fallen tree trunk, removed the map from within Hiccup's waistcoat and threw it to the Silver Phantom.

Oh for Thor's sake, thought Hiccup. *I really should have hidden that map a bit better. What was I thinking? Some undercover Outcast I am...*

In a pouring silver motion, the Silver Phantom caught the map in mid-air, and then shot up, up, out of the trees and away.

While Valhallarama was momentarily distracted,

Hiccup wriggled out of his waistcoat and ran out of reach. Valhallarama drew her sword, the mighty Nevermiss, with a great swaggering swish.

Hiccup drew his own sword.

He was beginning to feel a little hurt that she still hadn't recognised him. He was her *son*, after all. You'd have thought some kind of mother instinct might have kicked in by now.

But then Valhallarama really hadn't been around that much, thought Hiccup bitterly, trying to ignore the rising lump in his throat as he remembered how many times he'd written to her as a child asking for her to come back home for some reason or another, and how many times she'd written back to say how important her Quest was.

More important than me, thought Hiccup. *No wonder she doesn't recognise me. I haven't seen her in two years.*

Valhallarama lunged at him.

Hiccup met the lunge directly and replied with one of his own, rather more courteous and less deadly, but a joy of sword-work nonetheless.

He could see the surprise in Valhallarama's bright blue eyes above him, which was a source of satisfaction, however difficult the circumstances.

It is always gratifying when your mother realises you
are a worthy opponent.

Because swordfighting was the one thing he was
really gifted at. And over the past year he had had
pretty much twice-daily practice against people and
dragons who weren't just fooling around, they really
and truly hated him and wanted him dead.

So it was a hymn to the gods of war to watch
him now, like listening to a singer with the voice of
an angel.

Plus he was left-handed, and a good leftie always has an advantage over a good rightie.

However his faithful dragon companions weren't leaving anything to chance.

They had now arrived on the scene, and the Wodensfang, his eyes lit up with surprising excitement at the battle, considering his great age, shouted, 'Number 4, guys! Number 4!'

Number 4 was one of the many manoeuvres they had worked out during an exciting year of fighting in forests, among other places, and it was one of the more successful ones.

'Mfff, mfffff, mfff, mfff, mmmmmmmmmfffff!' shouted Hiccup desperately. (Which meant: 'Guys! Please, no, guys! We don't want to kill her! This is a big misunderstanding! She's my mother!')

But his dragons had absolutely no idea what he was saying, so they put Number 4 into action.

The Windwalker bounded around the two fighters, barking excitedly, to confuse them.

And then Toothless dive-bombed Valhallarama's head, biting into her metal arm (giving himself a gum-ache), while the Wodensfang set fire to the bottom of a tree just behind her.

Even Hiccup's incredible swordfighting skills

were challenged by this, because he was having to defend himself from Valhallarama while trying to manoeuvre her into a position out of the way of that tree when it fell down on top of her.

Oh for Thor's sake, this was impossible! That six-foot-three female metal mountain would just not budge.

He parried her lunges with a Grimbeard's Grapple, Flashburn Fancy and two Points of Order before realising she was *never* going to move, and for such a very small dragon the Wodensfang was making good progress with that tree trunk – it was already beginning to wobble, and visible flames were lighting up the grass at the bottom.

Desperately, Hiccup defended himself from the Nevermiss's most brilliant fencing-work with his left hand, while trying to yank off that horrible jammed-tight tin-can of a helmet with the other.

'TIM-BERRRRRR!' sang the Wodensfang and Toothless in joyful chorus together. The burnt-through tree was swaying madly.

Hiccup gave one last beyond-hope pull and the helmet finally shot off his head with a violence that made his ears tingle.

He shouted at the top of his voice, 'Mother!

Don't attack! It's only me, your son, Hiccup! And get out of the way of that tree, which is about to fall on your head!'

But *most* unfortunately, totally unconsciously, he shouted those words in the tongue he had been used to speaking in for the last year (he hadn't had any human companions you see). Not in Norse, but in Dragonese: 'Mi mamma! Na bitey! Issa lonely me, ta dissappointa Hiccup! Plus outadaway da leafdangle which yappen lowdown ta brain-boxer!'

So much for letting her know gently in a quiet moment.

Life is sometimes much more messy than that.

" Mi mamma ! Na bitey !.
Issa lonely me, ta dissapointa
Hiccup ! "

Valhallarama's blue eyes practically fell out of her visor, popping with amazement. She went absolutely rigid with shock, in the slightly ridiculous and undignified pose of Mid-Looping-Loot-Bubbles, one of Flashburn's more showy-off moves which should really only be attempted by someone about ten years younger and half the girth of Valhallarama, formidable action-woman though she was.

No wonder she was surprised.

For in one gob-smacked, sword-arm freezing second, she had learnt:

1. *That she had just been attempting to kill her only son by accident.*
2. *That said son was in fact the Outcast and Enemy of the Wilderwest, whom everybody (not just the witch) said was the one who set free the Dragon Furious and started this war between dragons and humans.*
3. *That the same son appeared to have the Slavemark on his forehead.*
4. *That the same son appeared to be fluent in Dragonese, a language that had been banned. Not that anyone but Hiccup could speak it anyway.*

This was a very great deal to take in, in just one moonlit moment.

The one piece of information that she wasn't able to take in, because it was spoken in Dragonese, was the one that would have been most immediately useful to her.

The information that a tree was about to fall on her head.

CRAAASSSHHHHH!

The tree snapped off at the trunk and...

BOOOOOIIIING!!!!

"T-T-TIMBER!!!"

… It landed plum on Valhallarama's metal head.

And then bounced off it on to the ground.

Valhallarama stood absolutely stock still for one second.

She re-arranged herself into a more dignified position.

And then she swayed gently on the spot…

And…

CRAAAASSHHHHH!!!

She went down like the tree trunk itself.

'N000000000000000000000!!!!!!!!!'

Oh dear, oh dear, oh dear!

Hiccup hopped anxiously from foot to foot.

'B-B-BINGO!' shouted Toothless. 'GOOD
SH-SH-SHOT WODENSFANG!'

And then he flapped down and shouted insults
down her visor.

'YOU B-B-BIG HUMAN BULLY!'

Hiccup tried to wave him out the way, and
Toothless thought he was reminding him about
manners.

'SORRY, YOU GREAT METAL
M-M-MOLLUSC! PARDON ME, YOU
LUMPING L-L-LARDBOTTOM LEADBELLY!
EXCUSE US, YOU TERRIFYING TIN
OF T-T-TESTOSTERONE!'

Lumping
L-L-LardBottom
LeadBelly!

'*Manners,*' said
Toothless smugly to Wodensfang.

'Yes, well done, Toothless,' congratulated the
Wodensfang brightly. '*Lovely apologising.*'

Hiccup pushed Toothless off and snapped open
his mother's visor.

Oh thank Thor, she's breathing…

She *was* breathing but she was out for the count,
and there was a big fat lump on the front of her
forehead. Unfortunately the Windwalker, seeing that
the terrifying Warrior was still breathing and whipped
up into a state of hysterical panic
by the fighting, tried to get
Hiccup to ride him out
of danger.

And when Hiccup wouldn't listen, he lost it entirely, and picked Hiccup up in his claws, despite him desperately struggling and shouting, '𝔑ooo!!! It's 𝔪𝔶 𝔪other!!! It's 𝔪𝔶 𝔪other!!!'

Wodensfang and Toothless flew on either side of his head making soothing noises, thinking that he was the one who had taken a funny turn on account of all the fighting.

It took him ten minutes to get through to them what had happened even without the helmet to shout through.

After catching their breath, Hiccup insisted that they went back to where he thought the fight had taken place, but there was no sign of any unconscious mother, just a deep indentation in the snow where she had fallen beside the still smouldering tree-trunk.

Where had she gone? Had the Razorwings got her? Or had the Silver Phantom returned and carried her to safety?

They searched the forest for the rest of that night, but they never found her.

Eventually in the early hours of the next morning, Hiccup pushed aside some brambles and crawled into a cave he had been using as a hide-out for some sleep. The warm wet shaggy body* of the

---

* The Windwalker is looking a little less shaggy because he has grown a little older.

Windwalker beside him, and his two friends Toothless and Wodensfang snuggled on his chest were always a source of comfort.

He might be an Outcast, but at least he had his dragons with him. Not like Fishlegs, who was entirely alone.

Just as he was falling asleep, Hiccup remembered something.

He no longer had the map.

3. HICCUP MUST DIE

The Wodensfang had in fact been right about the Dragon Furious sending a dragon to kill Hiccup.

A few weeks earlier, in the endless night of winter on the little isle of Berk, where the air was so cold it stung the skin like bees, the Dragon Furious lay in the smoking ashy remains of what had once been a Hooligan village.

The Dragon Furious was a Seadragonus Giganticus Maximus, and he was in command of the Dragon Rebellion. His aim was nothing less than the extinction of the entire human race.

The Hooligans had escaped from the last terrible dragon attack, fleeing to the islands of the south which were still holding out against the relentless progress of the dragon invaders, but leaving the island of Berk to a triumphant Dragon Furious.

The island of Berk was a new and important conquest for Furious. And yet...

And yet there was *one* Hooligan who had not been among the Hooligans who escaped from the island on this day. One Hooligan whom the Dragon Furious and the entire Dragon Rebellion had been hunting without success, over seas and forests and mountains, through ice caves and volcanoes...

Hiccup Horrendous Haddock the Third.

So many times had the little Hooligan slipped through Furious's talons at the very last minute, double-backing, sneaking past, and streaking away on the back of his Windwalker, with the whole howling pack of dragons after him, like a tricksy little fox fleeing the hunt.

Kneeling in front of the Dragon Furious was a rare Triple-header Deadly Shadow dragon. You could not see him, for a Deadly Shadow was one of those chameleon dragons whose skin can mirror any background or passing object, so at that moment he appeared to be invisible.

'Hiccup must die,' said the Dragon Furious to the Deadly Shadow. 'We have to catch him, or our cause is lost. Can *you* do it? Can you find and kill Hiccup where all others have failed?'

Slowly the camouflaged skin of the Deadly Shadow turned back to its natural colour, and it was as if the terrifying creature was suddenly materializing out of thin air. You could see him in all his splendour now: gleaming, muscled, panther-like strength, frighteningly efficient-looking claws and jaws that could shoot forth both lightning bolts and flame.

The three heads of the Shadow smiled. The poison-ducts in his six cheeks pulsed yellow for a second. Out of their secret hiding-places crept a bright, slitting talon or two that shone for a second and then slid back.

'My lord Furious,' said the middle head of the Deadly Shadow dragon. 'Once, my brothers and I loved a human. And this human died of grief because of the actions of her human family. Now we hate the human with a hatred strong as acid. If you ask us to kill him, the boy is as good as dead already.'

'Ah,' said the Dragon Furious with satisfaction. 'I knew I was right to choose you, for you are so like myself. I needed one who hates like I do, and who will not weaken, for the Hiccup boy, with his antics releasing all the dragon-traps, has even been gaining sympathy among the weaker members of my Rebellion. Follow him, and kill him. Hiccup must die!'

'And Hiccup *shall* die!' hissed the three heads of the Deadly Shadow.

He folded back his wings like a bat, and leapt into the air, turning white as the blizzard as soon as he hit the sky. The Dragon Furious watched him go, the quiet snow falling.

Seadragonus Giganticus Maximus

~ STATISTICS ~

FEAR FACTOR: 10
ATTACK: ……………………….. 10
SPEED: ………………………….. 10
SIZE: ………………………….. 10
DISOBEDIENCE: ……………….. 10

The largest of the dragon species,
Seadragonus Giganticus Maximus
live in the open ocean.

Learning to Speak Dragonese

Toothless's Guide to Being p-p-polite...

Moo-lady, yow snoddly sniffer is giganticus plus warticus, plus, warra eye-pleezee, fur-sprouty hug-dangles!

Madam, you have a very large and lovely spotty nose, and what beautiful hairy arms!

Toothless issa griefspotty me misschance f-f-flicka-flame ta gob-sprout. Twassa bigtime hiccup.

I am so sorry that I accidentally set fire to your beard, it was a total mistake.

WHOOPS!

T-t-toothless didn't mean to step in a Goredragon poo and tread it all over your floor...

Toothless mak ta me m-m-most speshally griefspotties. Toothless's runners pop in a cack-cack di Goredragon, plus me pressit muchwide ondi floorsheet.

I make you my most heartfelt apologies. I seem to have stepped in Goredragon poo and trodden it all over your carpet.

T-t-toothless goggla ta struggla wi munch-munch di saltsicks lonelywise. Teggly me adda.

I can see you are having trouble eating all those oysters on your own. Let me help you.

Ne-ah, Toothless na s-s-sporta da sprouty-warm. Ta maka me inta un girly-goo, plus me preffa ma flame-shootys coldover and me flip-flaps lendinta forkfreezies. Thankee par ta warmwishes.

No, I will NOT wear that furry coat. It makes me look like a sissy and I would rather my fire-holes froze up and my wings turned into ice-lollies. Thank you for your concern.

4. ONE OF HICCUP'S LESS BRILLIANT PLANS

A few weeks after losing the map, Hiccup Horrendous Haddock the Third was lying crouched in the reeds on the edges of a tiny little island right in the middle of the bay that stood in front of Prison Darkheart – the bay called *The Dragons' Graveyard*.

With him were the Windwalker, the Wodensfang and Toothless.

They were crouching down beside Hiccup, wings shivering, cats' eyes peering fearfully over the ferns at the horror of the landscape all around them.

'You are n-n-not going in there...' squeaked Toothless, pointing a horrified wing at Prison Darkheart.

'P-p-please tell Toothless you are not going in there...'

'I don't see that we have any choice,' said Hiccup bitterly, 'now that my mother has betrayed us. I must say, I know she's always been a bit absent, but I never thought she'd actually fight *against* me.'

Hiccup swallowed. The whole world was burnt to ashes, and here he was, feeling like crying over a wayward mother.

But there was no other explanation. Valhallarama must have got her Phantom to carry Grimbeard the Ghastly's map to the witch because the witch was now in Darkheart, hunting for the Dragon Jewel. And so too were the Meathead, Murderous, Visithug and Hooligan Tribes.

Hiccup had seen all the ships sail in over the past two weeks.

Which meant that Hiccup's friend Fishlegs was in there, and Hiccup's father, Stoick the Vast. And Hiccup was determined to get them out, now he knew where they were.

It's my fault they're in there, so I'm going to get them out...

'Oh shiver my t-t-talons!' wept poor Toothless, so terrified he fell off Hiccup's shoulder and into the

sea Hiccup was crouching in. 'Look!' He
pointed a wing at all the dragon corpses
lying in the sea around them. 'The
Dragon F-f-furious has been trying
to get in every night! How are
you going to get in if even
he hasn't managed it!'

PRISON
DARKHEART

At one end of the bay was the gigantic prison that formed the only entrance to the great walled hunting-grounds of the Amber Slavelands. The walls that encircled the Amber Slavelands were not, perhaps, as long as the Great Wall of China, but they were certainly much higher, and a similarly miraculous construction of the Ancient World.

In front of the prison, the tide was slowly sinking and gradually revealing the grotesque and pathetic shapes of thousands of dead dragons. Ancient dragon skeletons jutted from the waters of the bay like airy melancholy cathedrals, with seagulls shrieking through the long-dead ribcages.

And there were fresh dragon corpses too, smelling to high heaven, and leaking green blood into the water, because every night now, the prison was attacked by some of the most ferocious forces of the Dragon Rebellion.

'This is a terrible plan! The witch and Alvin will catch you!' squeaked Toothless, in an agony of fear.

'Nobody's going to catch us,' said Hiccup soothingly. 'We'll just sneak in, see if we can find my father and Fishlegs and the Jewel, and sneak out again. Us Outcasts are good at sneaking. And if anybody spots us, I've got the Slavemark, so they'll just think I'm another slave.

'And also,' he raised an eyebrow, 'I'm going to be wearing my cunning disguise.'

Hiccup had changed quite a bit after a year of living as an Outcast. He was thinner, taller, and his voice had deepened, and was unsteadily sliding all the time between a gruff and a squeak, so that was a disguise in itself.

Now he took off his helmet, and brought out a rag from his rucksack and wound it round his left eye like an eye patch. He fixed a piece of pink-ish candle wax right on the tip of his nose, and it made a rather convincing wart. And he smeared himself with some Stinkdragon stink, that he had been keeping in a little

Hiccup's Cunning disguise →

pot, after carefully extracting it from a hibernating Stinkdragon in the Flaming Forest a couple of days earlier.

The smell would stop people coming too close. 'How do I look?'

Toothless made his yuckiest 'yucky' face. 'T-t-toothless not want to come near you. Is very, very yucky.'

'Yes, well you don't have to come, Toothless, if you don't want to. It may be better if you didn't, because it's very dangerous for dragons in there,' said Hiccup. 'And I want you to be safe. You can stay here with the Windwalker.'

The Windwalker protested, 'What do you mean, stay here? I'm coming too.'

But Hiccup shook his head. 'I'm afraid you can't come, Windwalker. The Wodensfang and Toothless can hide down my waistcoat. But you're far too big to hide and they'll kill you if they spot you.'

The Windwalker shut his eyes and put his tail between his legs. All of his spines drooped.

smell so strong it was practically visible

77

We'll be back soon, Windwalker, I promise

Hiccup hugged him affectionately,
holding on to that warm shaggy familiar neck, smelling
his lovely smell as if it might be for the last time.

The Windwalker smelled
of drinking chocolate.

'Now, Windwalker, you must stay here and guard my helmet and the hide-out in the Forgotten Forest so that nobody finds it. We'll be back before you know it.'

Hiccup had been dreading this moment for a long time, because he knew that he might be about to see his father again. For Hiccup had inadvertently caused Stoick to be made an Outcast from his own Tribe, and turned from a Chief respected by all, with a comfortable life shouting out orders and eating a lot, to a life as a slave in the Amber Slavelands.

Hiccup loved and respected his father, and it was almost unbearable to think of Stoick the Vast in this position, particularly when it was all Hiccup's fault. Had the experience of slavery changed Stoick? What must he be thinking of Hiccup? And what about Fishlegs? Was he all right?

Thoughts like these were a kind of torment.

But sometimes the bravest thing a Hero has to do is not fighting monsters and cheating death and witches. It is facing the consequences of his own actions.

Hiccup *had* to do this.

'Toothless, are you coming, or staying?'

'Toothless will come,' said Toothless grandly,

pointing his wing at Hiccup, 'because you need my h-help and what would you do without me? C-c-can Toothless wear an eye patch too?'

'You don't need to wear an eye patch, Toothless. Nobody's going to see you.'

'Is quite c-c-cool though...'

'Toothless!'

Toothless dived down Hiccup's waistcoat with a squeal.

A slave-ship was making its way through the reeds, delivering fresh slaves to the ravenous maw of the Slavelands. It was hurrying, for the tide was sinking fast, and as soon as it was in, the Dragon Rebellion would attack, and if the ship was still there, they would all be dead men.

Hiccup took a deep breath, sank beneath the water, and swam after the ship. It was picking its way like a slalom through the dragon corpses.

Hiccup swam after it, the Wodensfang puffing

into his mouth to give him oxygen every now and then. Hiccup surfaced at the back of the ship and hitched a lift by driving two daggers into the wooden sides.

He could hear the snap of the whips of the slave-drivers above, the moans of the poor tired slaves as they groaned with the weariness of the long journey, and the splash of their oars.

The ship stopped and someone shouted up to the tiny figures way way up on the battlements.

CRREEEEEEEAAAAAAAAAAAAK!!!!

With a protesting shriek of wheels and pulleys, the terrible door of Traitor's Gate opened slowly.

Above the door, these ominous words were carved into the stone, each letter the height of a man:

FORGET ALL THOSE WHO ENTER HERE.

The slave-driver snapped the whip again and screamed the command to row.

Exhausted, the slaves rowed themselves through the door, and into their own oblivion.

Slowly, and with dreadful finality, the iron door slammed...

... shut.

The Windwalker, crouched in the reeds, let out a whine of anxiety as he saw it. He stayed there, shivering and alone, until a sentry on Prison Darkheart must have spotted him because there was a mighty blaze from the battlements, and something huge and heavy rocketed past the poor Windwalker's head and exploded into the reeds beside him.

What *was* that? What *were* these terrifying new weapons the humans were using against the dragons?

The Windwalker did not stay to find out. With a terrified squeal, he launched out of the rushes and flapped for his life on sad raggedy wings, flying north to the Forgotten Forest. He looked mournfully over his shoulders at the horror of Prison Darkheart.

But in the fear of the moment he left the stupid helmet with the feather on it behind in the reeds.

Many hours later, something came winding through the melancholy cathedrals of long-dead dragons' bones and landed next to the helmet and drank in the smell of it.

You couldn't see them, but the three heads of the camouflaged dragon smiled, and its talons sprang out like flick-knives.

'Hiccup...' hissed the middle head of the dragon with satisfaction. 'Hiccup, Hiccup, *Hiccup*. He mussst be in there.'

All three heads turned towards the Prison Darkheart. 'And now,' hissed the third head, 'now we have him trapped.'

'He seems,' said the third head, sniffing the helmet again and wrinkling his nose in disgust, 'to have had an encounter with a Stinkdragon that is going to make him laughably easy to track.'

The dragon took off in the direction of the prison, slowly flapping its wings and circling it like some greedy disguised vulture.

And we know who that dragon is, don't we? Because there aren't all that many three-headed invisibly-camouflaged dragons in the Archipelago.

It was the Deadly Shadow.

5. THE WRONG SIDE OF THE DOOR

Hiccup's not-so-brilliant plan went wrong right from the beginning.

The slaves on the ship on which he had hitched a lift were disembarking and slipping from under the gang-plank of the boat. Hiccup intended to melt into the shadows and explore the prison on his own. As an Outcast, he was now an expert at this kind of sneaky behaviour.

But as he tiptoed away, the Wodensfang sneezed from his waistcoat. It was quite a quiet sneeze, but unfortunately Toothless called out 'Bliss ta!' – which is Dragonese for 'Bless you!' – very, very loudly.

And then 'Bliss ta! Bliss ta! B-b-blissta!' as Wodensfang sneezed three more times.

The prison guard on the gang-plank heard the noise and looked under the gang-plank.

'WHERE D'YA THINK YOU'RE GOING?' yelled the guard, assuming he was an escaping slave. The guard gave him a crack of a whip sharper than the bite of a Squirrel-serpent, and invited him to join the long line of slaves sinking ankle deep into the sand as they disembarked from the ship.

'Toothless,' whispered Hiccup furiously, holding on to his stinging shoulder as he shuffled down a maze of corridors into the dark belly of the prison's central courtyard. 'Please be quiet. Remember, we're Outcasts... spies...'

'T-t-toothless was being polite!' protested Toothless.

'Yes, I know, politeness is good. Politeness is very good. I'm really impressed by your politeness, it's just if you could keep your politeness quite quiet at the moment, I'd be very grateful...'

Chaos reigned in the prison courtyard.

Hiccup looked around with his mouth open. It was as if he had stepped through the door into another, grimmer world.

Long lines of tables with people sitting eating at them seemed to suggest that this was some sort of open-air dining room. The people were of all ages from six or seven upward, and had the S of the Slavemark on their foreheads.

But around these people eating was the manic din of war, and the sheer mad noise of it caused ears to ring as if an orchestra in Valhalla had turned up the volume to 'extra loud'.

Screaming warriors ran hither and thither,

hammering swords and spears out of molten red-ended metal. Above Hiccup's head, continuous rocket explosions sent out huge clouds of yellow smoke that stung his eyelids and crept inside his nose like sulphurous slugs, gagging his throat with the smell of rotten eggs.

Lying around the place were enormous evil-looking dragon-traps, weird crazy inventions such as catapults that launched thirty-five spears at once, and Northbows that did the same with arrows. It was all so noisy you couldn't hear yourself think.

The guard shoved them all in there, before hurrying off, bellowing at them over his shoulder to 'Eat well for the Seeking begins soon!' – whatever *that* might mean. To Hiccup's horror, the courtyard was absolutely packed to the brim with people he knew, from Tribes all over the Archipelago, and as he was the most Wanted person in the Wilderwest right now, he thought it would be wise to slide away into a side corridor.

But things really weren't going Hiccup's way this morning.

'HOY! YOU OVER THERE! SMELLY BOY! COME AND JOIN US AT OUR TABLE!' shouted a large fat man from a table nearby.

Hiccup jumped guiltily.

And then he realised, in total amazement, that the large fat man shouting at him was in fact his own father, Stoick the Vast.

It was the moment Hiccup had been dreading.

The wart and the eye-patch and the smell were doing their job though, because Stoick clearly hadn't the faintest idea who he was.

'HOY! SMELLY BOY!' yelled Stoick again. 'GET OVER HERE QUICK OR ALL THE FOOD WILL BE GONE!'

Slowly, Hiccup walked up to the table where Stoick was sitting.

As he sat down, all the others at the table moved gently away from him like a sea parting, their noses wrinkling.

This must be what it's like to have a highly infectious disease, thought Hiccup.

Stoick grunted and pushed a large chunk of bread and a big handful of mussels at Hiccup, trying not to breathe in Hiccup's particularly ripe and luscious stink. 'Eat up, boy, before I change my mind.'

At least his father was looking well.

He looked a little sad around the eyes perhaps, with a few streaks of grey in his magnificent moustache

and he'd lost a bit of weight, but he could still be described as 'a hugely fat man with a beard as red and out of control as a forest fire'.

And to Hiccup's passionate relief, Stoick seemed to be in some sort of position of importance and respect among the slaves, or at least in the group seated at this particular table.

Stoick the Vast (once the proud chief of the Hooligan Tribe, now a SLAVE)

Once a Chief, always a Chief.

'New boy, eh?' said Stoick, as Hiccup helped himself. 'What's your name, kid?'

Hiccup forced himself to look his father right in the eye.

This was awful.

He was in two minds about this, because he was undercover of course, and it would be deadly dangerous if people started recognising him, but surely, *surely*, Stoick must know who he was?

Valhallarama was away questing a lot, so she had some sort of excuse. But Stoick and Hiccup had sat together every single day at the breakfast table for thirteen years!

How unmemorable exactly *was* he? For Thor's sake, he knew he'd grown up a little but it wasn't as if he was wearing a large curly false moustache or anything.

But no, Stoick clearly hadn't a clue, not even the merest smidgeon of an idea that the boy he was sharing his supper with was his own only son.

'My name is… Warty McSmelly,' said Hiccup.

'Good name,' said Stoick approvingly. 'What Tribe were you, before the Slavemark?'

'The Lost Tribe,' said Hiccup, thinking fast.

'Welcome to the Company of Amber-Hunters, Warty McStinky,' bellowed Stoick, giving him a hearty slap on the back.

'Mc*Smelly*,' Hiccup corrected him, choking slightly on his mussel.

'You have to belong to a group here, McSmelky.'

'*Smelly*...' Oh for Thor's sake, his father couldn't even remember his fake name! He was going to forget it himself at this rate.

'Otherwise you won't last a day out there on the Sands,' bellowed Stoick importantly. 'We are the Amber-Hunters. Listen up, Amber-Hunters! We have a new boy here! This is Portly McSpelly, late of the Lost Tribe.'

Hiccup looked at the Amber-Hunters and then around him at the courtyard, and his heart sank right down into his sandals.

Everything was back to front and upside down. All the wrong people were in charge. Up at the High Table were the Warriors of the Wilderwest, swaggering around in their purple and yellow sashes, and amongst them Hiccup recognised some of the more unpleasant Hooligans from his own Tribe, the new chief, Snotface Snotlout, and his cronies Dogsbreath the Duhbrain and Clueless.

And down here in the Slave-Pit were many, many noble, respected men and women, who a year earlier were proud Warriors of their Tribes, and were now wearing the Slavemark.

Many were Peaceables, Grim-bods, Quiet-Lifes. But here on Stoick's own table, in his Company of Amber-Hunters, among the Silents and the Bashem-Oiks, were one or two Hooligans that Hiccup knew well. The Vicious Twins. Hodgepodge the Loony.

And Gobber the Belch, Hiccup's old teacher.

Gobber the Belch was a most respected Warrior who had fought bravely for his Tribe on numerous occasions and was, once upon a lifetime away, in charge of the Pirate Training Programme on Berk.

Hiccup had a great lump in his throat as Gobber looked up and wished him a kindly hello, and he saw the horrible 'S' on his teacher's forehead.

Who had done this to him? How dare they!

And to make matters worse, even Gobber didn't recognise him. Had he really changed that much?

Lonelier even than he had felt as an Outcast, Hiccup looked around the table, and around the whole courtyard.

He was looking for Fishlegs, and Fishlegs didn't seem to be there.

'Um… Stoick the Vast, sir,' said Hiccup politely. 'Is there a boy called Fishlegs in the Company of the Amber-Hunters?'

Stoick looked uncomfortable and sad.

'Fishlegs?' he said. 'No, I've never heard of a boy called Fishlegs, have you, Gobber?'

Gobber the Belch shook his head. 'No, I've never heard that name before, either.'

Never heard of Fishlegs?

What were they talking about?

Fishlegs had been memorably bottom of absolutely everything in Gobber's Pirate Training Programme for about five years – Bashyball, Badd Speling, the lot.

Gobber used to say that he was going to get Fishlegs up to Warrior status or die in the attempt. Hiccup's father had spent most of Hiccup's life a little annoyed that Hiccup had such a little weirdo as a friend. How could they possibly say they'd never even heard of him?

There was something very odd going on round here.

Hiccup was about to ask another question when Snotface Snotlout, the new Chief of the Hooligan Tribe, came strolling up to the table.

SNOTLOUT

Snotlout was
looking in excellent
shape.

If he hadn't been
such an unpleasant
character, it would
have been a pleasure
to see him come into
his own like this.

Snotlout had always
wanted to be a Chief and now
that Fate had given him his dearest
wish he was loving every second of it.

In the sunshine of everyone's admiration, he
seemed to have grown about a foot. He swaggered
around, joking with his friends,
glowing with a new relaxed
consequence.

'Nice fighting against the
dragons yesterday, Snotty!'
called out one of Snotlout's
mates, Vandal the Visithug.
'How many did you kill,
was it nine?'

'I think it was eleven,'

Stoick the Vast

beamed Snotlout carelessly. 'But everyone did well.'

So when Snotlout strolled over to the Amber-Hunters' table, his words were not, at the start at least, deliberately intended to offend, because Snotlout was in a very good mood.

It was just that Snotlout was not accustomed to thinking about the feelings of anyone other than a certain Snotface Snotlout.

'Eat up there, guys,' was all Snotlout said, smiling, off-hand.

But Stoick and Gobber and Baggybum *did take offence*. They flinched at the casual command given by one who was so much their junior; one who was Baggybum's son, Stoick's nephew and Gobber's pupil, and who should be showing them considerably more respect, particularly since the reversal of fortune on both sides.

Hiccup could not really look at the hurt expression on their faces and the sad sinking of their shoulders.

Gobber the Belch

Baggybum the Beerbelly

This was the world turned upside-down indeed.

'Snotlout,' asked Hiccup, hurriedly changing the subject, 'have you seen a boy called Fishlegs anywhere here?'

'It's *Chief* Snotlout to you, slave,' Snotlout corrected, instantly guarding his dignity, his good mood fading. *He* didn't recognise Hiccup either, flicking his eyes over him dismissively, wrinkling his gigantic nose at the smell. 'Yes, Fishlegs is one of the Lost – he disappeared in the Seeking a couple of weeks ago. Not before time, he was a total weed. Nothing worth bothering about. A bit of a weakling like you, but without the powerful pong.'

Nothing worth bothering about…

Baggybum the Beerbelly carefully put down his spoon. He looked at his son and quietly said the words that Hiccup most dreaded his own father would say to *him*.

'Snotlout,' said Baggybum the Beerbelly, 'I am ashamed to be your father.'

Snotlout turned white, shocked. For just one instant, he shrank in front of their eyes and became the small boy he once was, standing in front of his father, his uncle, his teacher – the three men whose approval he most desperately sought.

And then Snotlout composed himself, put on his arrogance once again, and narrowed his eyes for the fight.

'You have no reason to say that. I may have made that runt Fishlegs a slave, but I did not make *you* slaves. You did that to yourselves, by not showing our King Alvin enough respect.'

'We acted out of loyalty to Stoick. But you did not try to intervene with our so-called King Alvin on our behalf, did you, Snotlout?' said Gobber thoughtfully.

'Why should I when you act like fools?' snorted Snotlout.

'Ashamed of *me*? I should be ashamed of you, and you should be proud that I am a Chief. *You* were never a Chief, Baggy, were you?' sneered Snotlout. 'You were not really Chief material.'

He patted his father on the shoulder and sauntered off.

OK, so this wasn't all right. This wasn't all right at all.

Hiccup's hand was shaking as he picked up his mussel and continued eating.

Lost in the Seeking? What did that mean?
Where on earth was Fishlegs?

A little girl in a bear-suit, called Eggingarde ↓

A little girl was sitting beside him, with huge doom-y eyes, a bear-suit with all the buttons done up in the wrong button-holes and very dark straggly hair that stuck straight out of her head at odd angles. She seemed to read his mind.

'Shh,' said the little girl. A lot of her teeth had recently fallen out and she was very serious for such a small person. 'We're not allowed to talk about the Lost. It's not good for morale.'

Lost????? What do you mean, Lost?????

But now the little girl said in an interested fashion, 'Warty McSmelly, your waistcoat is on fire.'

Aaagh!

Hiccup looked down,
and there, indeed, was grey smoke
drifting out of the top of his waistcoat. Toothless,
who had been scratching away at Hiccup's tummy in
an I-need-food sort of way for the past five minutes,
had given up waiting, and was now resorting to the
desperate tactic of sending up smoke signals.

Hiccup clamped his waistcoat to his chest to stop
more smoke coming up. What possible excuse could
he have for his waistcoat being on fire?

Eventually he spluttered, 'Must have got caught
by a spark from one of those explosions out in the
courtyard... don't worry! I've put it out now!'

And then in one desperate swoop Hiccup
picked up the last of the bread, cheese and mussels

and pretended, slightly theatrically, to drop one of the mussels on the floor ('Whoops!') and dived under the table...

... where he took Toothless and the Wodensfang out of his waistcoat, scolding Toothless in a furious gritted-teeth whisper. 'Toothless, you must not set fire to my waistcoat! If anybody found out I had dragons on me, you would be *dead*.'

'Was an accident,' lied Toothless. 'Hunger makes Toothless's fireholes leak...'

'Now, Toothless,' whispered Hiccup, showing him the mussels and bread that he held in his clenched fist. 'There's not much to go round so before I give these to you remember your *manners*... Be polite... *Share*... Leave some for Wodensfang too.'

In the darkness of Prison Darkheart, it is even more important than usual to keep up your standards.

Toothless nodded his head, repeating, 'Oh yessee, yessee, me coglet, Toothless will share... Toothless very p-p-polite...'

Hiccup opened his hand.

Toothless opened his mouth so wide and moved so quick that he misjudged his lunge, and wrapped his little gums not just around the mussels, cheese and bread, but around *Hiccup's entire hand*.

Which was of course too big for him to swallow. Hiccup looked down at him in disbelief.

Goodness gracious, you wouldn't have thought that a dragon so small would be able to open his mouth that wide.

Slowly, with his tail stuck between his legs and his huge eyes apologetic, Toothless backed off the hand, leaving the food there.

'W-w-wodensfang first,' said Toothless piously, pretending that had not just happened. And he let the Wodensfang have a couple of dainty little picks before charging in to gobble up the lot.

'S-s-sorry, mussels,' said Toothless, with his mouth full. 'S-s-sorry, bread... Sorry cheese...'

'Yes, lovely apologising, Toothless,' whispered Hiccup, 'but you don't really have to apologise to your food... Although it's a nice idea, Toothless, don't get me wrong.'

Suddenly there was absolute dead silence in the great hall.

All the chattering ceased in a moment, like when small delicious furry animals freeze into quietness when wolves enter the wood.

And then, as he was crouched under the table, with the Wodensfang and Toothless eating mussels on the ground beside him, there came a sound that made Hiccup's neck crawl with fear as if beetles had crept underneath his collar, and every single individual hair on his head spike upwards as though they were the quills of a porcupine…

Step TAP, step TAP, step TAP, step TAP…

… along the floor of the suddenly silent courtyard.

And with a cold trickle of dread, Hiccup saw from underneath the table, the legs of a man come striding into view and stop right in front of him, so close that he could have reached out and touched them.

To be more precise, one leg was made out of flesh.

The other was made out of ivory.

Sadly Hiccup could not see the rest of him, for Alvin the Treacherous, King-in-Waiting of the Wilderwest, was a handsome sight indeed, a villain in the very flower and blossom of his villainy, blooming with warts like a tree in fruit, skeleton and snake tattoos writhing gloriously over his gigantic muscles and all the remaining parts of him that were still human.

Alvin the Treacherous
(King-in-Waiting) →

Which was not as many parts as the rest of us have, for Alvin was currently missing an arm, a leg, a nose and an eye, all replaced with splendid attachments made of the very best ivory, gold and iron that a King-in-Waiting could lay his hook on in the middle of a war.

Behind the tapping and the ticking of Alvin's progress across the courtyard, was a horrible rustling sound, like rats scuttling, and there was something running across the floor like a big white bony dog.

It wasn't a dog.

It was a witch as white as bone.

Alvin's horrible mother, the witch Excellinor ↑

A witch that walked on all fours like an animal.

The witch Excellinor, Alvin the Treacherous's mother.

Her poisoned iron fingernails scraping on the flagging, made that rat-scratch of a sound.

She stopped dead in front of Hiccup.

And then slowly, like an automaton, she turned her head.

And stared... right into Hiccup's eyes.

6. THE WITCH EXCELLINOR IS A LITTLE ANNOYED

OH FOR THOR'S SAKE.

Hiccup's heart melted within his chest as the witch's hollow eyes looked straight at him. She was like a living skeleton, a shock of hair streaming out behind her, all human kindness dead within her. Twenty years of living in the darkness of a tree trunk had bleached all the light out of her, and she was whiter than a slug, and meaner than a snake, and bowled into a hoop by the prison of the trunk.

They were caught red-handed.

She had been tearing up the Wilderwest in her hunt for this very same boy for the past year.

And there Hiccup was,
under the table not two feet
away from her quivering white
nose, frozen in the act of feeding
two banned dragons, both of them
hovering, petrified, in mid-air.

The witch sniffed once, twice.

'Dragons...' she hissed in horror.
'Dragons...'

She looked straight at him, and barked
like a dog.

But the witch was so blind she could
barely see a foot in front of her nose.

She did not see them.

At that distance she could only sense
movement.

Don't move, Toothless, thought Hiccup,
teeth gritted in terror. *Don't move...*

The witch carried on looking at them
for what seemed like a lifetime.

And then her long pointed nose, sharp as a knife, sniffed in disgust.

'That's weird,' said the witch dismissively. 'I thought I smelt dragons but it's just Slaves. They smell disgusting.'

And scuttle, scuttle, off she bounded, followed by the step TAP, step TAP of Alvin.

Thank Thor for the Stinkdragon stink.

Shaking with relief, Hiccup stuffed the Wodensfang back into his waistcoat.

The wart on the end of his nose fell off and he only just got to it in time because Toothless was about to eat it. Thoroughly rattled, he fastened it back on, put Toothless in his waistcoat with the Wodensfang, and popped back up to the top of the table.

The girl with the black hair and the big eyes was now sitting where he had been sitting.

Oh dear, those big doom-y eyes were rather alarming, they gave him quite a shock.

'You've been under there for a really long time,' said the girl solemnly.

'Yes, well, I was resting,' said Hiccup, feeling a little desperate.

'My name's Eggingarde,' said the little girl.

'Pleased to meet you, Eggingarde,' said Hiccup,

shaking her hand in a slightly frazzled way.

'Eggingarde, what is this Seeking thing, and how do you get Lost?'

'Us slaves of the Amber Slavelands go out on the Seeking every day,' said Eggingarde. She spoke in a very grown-up way for such a very little girl. 'At the first hint of low tide the bugle sounds and out we go on to the red sands, to seek the amber Jewel that the witch and her son Alvin are looking for, the one that is not there. For I have been out on the sands every day since I can remember, and I can tell you the Jewel is not there.'

Oh, great.

'Then the second bugle sounds,' said Eggingarde, in a scared deep whisper, 'and we return to Prison Darkheart. Unless...'

'Unless?'

'We are taken by the tide or...' Eggingarde stopped and opened her eyes even wider,
'... *something else.*'

Something about Eggingarde's doom-y eyes reminded Hiccup of someone, but he didn't know who.

'Eggingarde?' asked Hiccup. 'How long have you been in this prison?'

'For as long as I can remember,' replied Eggingarde.

Poor Eggingarde.

For as long as she could remember.

That was a long time.

'It's OK,' said Eggingarde. 'I'm not scared, because I am a Wanderer, and Wanderers are *wild*.'

Eggingarde pulled up the hat of her bearsuit, held up her ten fingers and made them into claws, making a hissing sound.

Hisssssss . . . .

Wanderers are WILD...

Hiccup pretended to be frightened and Eggingarde looked pleased.

Sometimes I even SCARE myself...

She carefully pulled down the hood of her bearsuit and whispered confidingly, 'Sometimes I even scare *myself*...'

'I bet you do,' said Hiccup admiringly. 'You didn't, by any chance, have a very scary grandmother, did you?'

'All Wanderer grandmothers are scary,' replied Eggingarde.

The witch leapt on to the Top Table, and when she straightened and opened her mouth to speak, it was as surprising as if a dog had suddenly got on its hind-quarters, and spoken like a human being.

'FOOLS!' screeched the witch.
'IGNORAMUSES! COWARDS! LAZYBONES! WHERE IS MY JEWEL, YOU NUMBSKULLS?'

'As you can see,' purred Alvin, polishing his hook, 'my mother is a little annoyed.'

'Slaves of the Amber Slavelands,' said the witch, calming down with bewildering swiftness, to the relief of her electrified audience.

Now she put on her sweetest, most reasonable voice. 'I have brought you Grimbeard's map.' She pointed at the map, which Hiccup could now see had been hung very carefully in the centre of the courtyard. 'See how clearly it is marked, how the Dragon Jewel is hidden somewhere in between the Maze of Mirrors, and the prison of Darkheart? All I ask, and it is for the good of the Wilderwest, is for you to find me the Jewel.

'But I see you may need a little more motivation. Listen up slaves!' yelled the witch. 'Anybody who finds me the Dragon Jewel, or indeed that little Outcast…' Hiccup gave a guilty jump in his seat to hear himself personally mentioned, but luckily everyone was concentrating so firmly on the witch that they did not notice. 'Whoever is the Jewel-finder gets the most precious prize of all…

'The prize,' crooned the witch, 'is FREEDOM.'

The crowds leaned forward eagerly, as if her words were water and they could drink them in. 'Freedom…' they crooned after her longingly. 'Freedom…'

'Just close your eyes,' smiled that infernal witch, 'and imagine what freedom means to you…'

Close your eyes and imagine what freedom means to you.

Such simple words.

The tattered scarecrow slaves closed their eyes and to each one it meant something different, but somehow the same. A clear blue sky. Flying on the back of a dragon. Out in a ship on the restless wave. A small house in a quiet village on a small island, with the smoke rising lazily from the chimney. Home.

Somewhere far away from these chains, these

desperate sands, these dark prison walls.

'What about the Slavemark?' cried out a slave, forgetting his place.

'It can be burnt off,' said the witch craftily. 'It's a slightly painful operation, but a small price to pay for FREEDOM.'

'You're lying aren't you, Mother?' whispered Alvin the Treacherous.

'Of course I'm lying,' the witch whispered back sweetly. 'The Slavemark can never be removed. Once a slave, always a slave.'

She turned back to the crowds of slaves.

'At the Seeking tomorrow, you shall bring me the Jewel, I know you shall!'

And she bounded off the table and out of the room.

Oh, that witch.

She and her son were *not* nice people.

Not nice people at all.

the key

the ticking-thing

Alvin had **EIGHT** of the **King's Lost Things**.

the Throne

the Crown

the ruby heart's stone

the sword

the shield

the arrow

7. A TRULY SCARY BEDTIME STORY – DO NOT READ THIS IF YOU ARE ABOUT TO GO TO BED

The little dark-haired girl called Eggingarde showed Hiccup where to sleep, in a corner of one of the dungeons of Prison Darkheart, which served as the slaves' dormitory.

'It looks like someone's already sleeping there,' said Hiccup doubtfully.

'No,' the little girl shook her head firmly and mournfully. 'It used to be Loserkid's bed. But he doesn't sleep there any more.'

Hiccup settled the Wodensfang and Toothless in the bed underneath a tattered blanket he had brought with him in his rucksack. He then had a whispered argument with Toothless under the blanket. 'What have I said, Toothless, about not eating inedible objects? Look, you've eaten a large hole out of my shirt...'

Toothless widened his greengage eyes, and innocently batted those preposterously long eyelashes.

'Wasn't T-t-toothless...' he mumbled in between a large mouthful of shirt, and he pointed a hopeful wing at the Wodensfang. 'Must have been the W-w-wodensfang...'

'I can see you're eating it right now!' whispered Hiccup in exasperation. 'You might as well own up!'

Toothless protested. 'No, n-n-no, no...'

But as he did so...

... he accidentally spat out one of the buttons. Both Hiccup and Toothless looked at the button. Even Toothless had the grace to look slightly guilty.

'S-s-sorry, shirt,' said
Toothless. 'Look, T-t-toothless
owned up!'

Toothless swallowed the remains
of the mouthful of shirt. 'Sorry, b-b-
belt. Sorry, top-of-trousers. Sorry, w-w-
waistcoat pocket... Ooh, Toothless is g-g-
good at this owning-up business...'

Hiccup sighed.

At this rate he was going to have nothing left that
didn't have bite marks in it.

Hiccup popped up from underneath the blanket
to ask Eggingarde a question.

'Where does Loserkid sleep now then?' asked
Hiccup.

Eggingarde frowned.

She didn't answer the question, she just counted
on her fingers the previous occupants of the bed
Hiccup was about to sleep in.

'And before Loserkid, it was Goggle-eyed
Gertie's, and before that it was the funny looking kid
with the big ears, and then there was Bobblehands –
that's his candle you're holding on to there.'

Hiccup took his hands off the candle as if it
was poisoned.

'And Littlearms the Brave and—'

'What happened to all these people?' asked Hiccup in horror.

Eggingarde did not answer.

'Are you quite sure that there was never a boy called Fishlegs sleeping in this bed?' asked Hiccup.

Eggingarde looked startled.

'Was Fishlegs a tall skinny boy with curly hair, smashed glasses and a face like a haddock who wanted to be a bard, just like me?'

'Yes,' said Hiccup eagerly. 'That's Fishlegs!'

'No,' said Eggingarde. 'I don't think I've ever seen anybody like that around here. But if I had,' she added wistfully, 'I think I would have liked him.'

'Eggingarde, you just described him!' said Hiccup in exasperation. 'You must have met him! Please, you have to tell me. He's my very great friend – what happened to him, where is he?'

Anxiously, Eggingarde shook her head. 'Sshh, I can't tell you. I'm not allowed to tell you about the Lost, it's bad for morale.'

She looked over her shoulder at the dungeon filled with whispering that was dying away as people settled down for the night.

Eggingarde put up the hood of her bearsuit, and

119

peered out from underneath.

'But I can tell you a story,' said Eggingarde determinedly, drawing down her thick dark eyebrows into a straight line and sucking in the air through the gap in her teeth. 'A very scary story.

'This story isn't about your friend Fishlegs.' Eggingarde shook her head violently. 'No, no, no, no, no. It's about... somebody else. The story is called: *The Slave-Boy, the Slave-Girl and the Monster of the Amber Slavelands.*'

POUF! Someone blew out the last candle in the dungeon, and in a doomy alarmed and alarming whisper, the little girl insisted on telling the story.

You have to imagine this story being told in the huge, echoing dungeon with the whispering voices in it sounding like spirits of the dead. You have to imagine Eggingarde, lying back in her bearsuit, conjuring up the story with wild wavings of her arms, and the moonlight making shadows of those arms on the dungeon walls.

THE STORY OF THE SLAVE-BOY, THE SLAVE-GIRL, AND THE MONSTER OF THE AMBER SLAVELANDS

'Once upon a time, a poor slave-boy and a slave-girl were paddling their sand-yachts in the most Evil of the Evil Reaches, deep in the heart of the Amber Slavelands,' began Eggingarde.

'Oh d-d-on't let her tell this story...' moaned Toothless from under the bedclothes. 'Toothless is worried that this might be a scary story and this is really quite a scary dungeon already...'

But Eggingarde was not to be stopped. She told the story as if she could not help herself from telling it, as if it was something that she could not keep to herself.

And Hiccup wanted to hear it, because he was worried that Eggingarde might be lying, and that this was a story about Fishlegs after all.

For someone so little, Eggingarde told an excellent story, as if she were a grown-up. Maybe it was the amount of time she spent with adults, or maybe it was just that Wanderers are wonderful storytellers.

'So low was the tide,' whispered Eggingarde, 'that the dreaded red sands stretched as far as the eye could see to the north, west, south and east – nothing but sand.

'Sand everywhere.

'Sand and a sinister silence.

'No birds called over those dreadful red sands. No seagulls screeched. For something terrible lurked beneath, something truly awful, and the birds knew to stay away.

'The slave-boy and the slave-girl paddled their sand-yachts out on the Eastern Sands, looking around with wild eyes, paddling as if witches were after them, though not a human soul could be seen in any direction. They kept looking left and right, and every now and then they stopped, reached down with their curious long nets, and bent to pick up a piece of amber lying on the beach.

'These pieces of amber, revealed by the low tide, were amber jewels of astonishing richness and variety, some the colour of honey and the lightness of air, others milky drops of yellow-green, others red as coral, warm to the touch and flecked with insects' wings.

'The Amber Slavelands are the best amber hunting-grounds in the whole of the Viking world, and many a slave has died there in the Quest to find the amber Jewel that would be fit for a warrior Viking princess, or the sword-hilt of a king. Low tide was best for finding amber, and lowest tide the best of all… But it was also the most dangerous.

'On, on, they paddled wildly. On and on and further out – the willow baskets on their backs nearly full now. The red sand made a sludgy swishing sound as the rims of the yachts splashed through it, on, on, on, for there was no turning back – and suddenly they stopped, both at exactly the same time, as sharply as if they had been hit by arrows.

'In front of them in the soft, wet, red sands were deep scarlet indentations appearing out of nowhere, and stretching out for miles, the sea puddling in the imprints, shining in the early evening sunset as if it were blood.

'The footprints were so large that the slave-girl's yacht came to a dull squelching stop right in the middle of one, and it was as large as the yacht itself.

'They were the footsteps…

'… of a GIGANTIC…

'… dragon.'

Toothless let out an unhappy whine.

'The slave-boy and the slave-girl felt their hearts almost die within them.

'Oh their luck had really vanished now.

'They knew that they were doomed.

'They looked at each other, and then they both hid their heads in their hands, curled up in the yachts, and the slave-boy pretended he was back home, in his village, and the slave-girl would have pretended she was back home if she had known where "home" was.

'But then the slave-boy remembered that he had been a Viking-in-Training, once upon a time, before he had been a slave. And the slave-girl remembered she was actually extremely brave.

'And the slave-girl and the slave-boy made fists out of their hands and shook them at the footprints to show defiance.'

Eggingarde made a fist out of her own hand, and shook it furiously in the air, and her shadow-fist shook, larger still, on the dungeon wall.

'Toothless not liking this story,' whispered Toothless.

'Yes, I don't think I like this story, either,' said Hiccup out loud, forgetting that Toothless wasn't supposed to be there.

'I don't have to tell you the end of the story if you don't want me to,' said Eggingarde, dropping her arms.

Oh dear, Hiccup had to hear the end of the story now, although he did not really want to hear it. 'No, carry on,' said Hiccup.

'The slave-girl and the slave-boy knelt to examine the footprint,' said Eggingarde. 'And very, very quietly, as they knelt, something *moved* in the sand behind them.

'It made no sound,
just a little light spurt of sand, like
a tiny, bubbling upwards waterfall. Up it rose
a little more. What was it? Something very curious…

'It was an *eye*, lying on the sand, blinking there
quietly for a moment, like it had been discarded by a
giant. Slowly, up it rose, and there were four more eyes
burrowing out of the sand like periscopes, curiously
attached to the end of long dragon fingers. And the five
together made a gigantic dragon claw.

'The claw held still. The eyes, horrifyingly
attached to the fingers, focused in on the boy without
blinking.

'And
kneeling in the
sand, they sensed a
presence
behind them,
the hairs on
the back of
their necks tingled
and prickled with
alarm, slowly they
peered behind
them—'

'You're freaking me out, Eggingarde,' said Hiccup.

'She's freaking me out too,' said the Wodensfang, peering out from under the covers.

'And T-t-toothless,' said Toothless, whose wings were over his ears. 'Can't you make her stop? B-b-bite her or something?'

'Manners,' said the Wodensfang.

'Just a l-l-little bite?' pleaded Toothless. 'A sweet one? To make her stop!'

But nothing was going to make Eggingarde stop now.

'"Aaaaargghhhhhhhhh!" they screamed,' said Eggingarde, and she sat up and screamed 'Aarraghhhh!' herself so loud, that Hiccup was astonished that none of the other slaves woke up, but they had obviously had a hard day out on the sands, for they snored on.

'And the slave-girl and the slave-boy got on their yachts, and propelled them forward with the oars as fast as they could.

'Wildly they oared the careering
yachts, crying and splashing across the
scarlet sand. They could not stop to blow their
whistles, they could not stop for the dragon was
after them, and if they stopped it would already be
too late for someone to save them.

'The dragon-claw-eye-periscope had
disappeared, but over their terrified shoulders
they could see five little humps of sand following
them, keeping pace with them, unhurried.'

Eggingarde's hands got more and more
excitable as she conjured up this nightmare, as
if she were conducting a savage piece of music,
faster and faster.

'The slave-boy and the slave-girl
oared on, and the five little humps of sand
followed, always keeping pace, patiently
waiting for them to tire.

'The slave-boy and the slave-girl oared
their yachts for what seemed like hours. There
was nowhere to go, no trees to climb, no one
to hear. The sands went on for ever.

'And then!'

And then???? Hiccup and Toothless and
Wodensfang leant forward, in horror…

Eggingarde swallowed, her arms momentarily
frozen, before carrying on, her voice even deeper.

'Out in the most eastern part of the Evil
Reaches, right by the rock that looked like a witch's
finger pointing upwards at the sky, the boy's yacht

caught on the metal edge of a dragon-trap, lying half covered in sand, waiting to catch dragons.

'The dragon-trap snapped shut, and caught the rim of the yacht, and held it fast.

'The boy's yacht tipped over, and smashed into the sand.

'And the boy gave up, he lay down on the sand and curled up into a little ball.

'The sands around him were quiet.

'Slowly, carefully, rose the dragon claw with the dreadful eyes on the end, burrowing out of the sand by the boy's foot.

'The boy did not move.

'And then the claw closed around his ankle and gently pulled him down below the sand.'

SOME STORIES
DO NOT HAVE
HAPPY
ENDINGS...

There was a long, long silence as Eggingarde's arms slowly dropped down to her sides.

'What happened to the slave-girl?' asked Hiccup, horrified.

'She carried on, back to the prison,' sighed Eggingarde.

Eggingarde pulled down the hood of her bearsuit.

Underneath the bedclothes, Toothless and the Wodensfang gave soft, unhappy whines. They obviously hadn't enjoyed the story either.

'That's a very, very sad story,' said Hiccup. 'Doesn't the boy get away? Couldn't you make the boy get away, and give the story a happy ending?'

'If I was living in a happier place,' said Eggingarde, 'I might tell stories with happier endings.'

Hiccup was getting a very, very bad feeling about this story.

'It wasn't a true story, was it, Eggingarde?' asked Hiccup.

Please don't let it be a true story...

Eggingarde said nothing.

'It wasn't about Fishlegs? The slave-boy and the slave-girl, they weren't you and Fishlegs, were they, Eggingarde?'

The dark was filled with silence.

'I can't tell you that,' said Eggingarde. 'It's bad for morale.'

Hiccup begged her and begged her, but she would not say another word.

It was dark. It was quiet. Everybody else was sleeping now.

A few moments later, snores came from the bed beside Hiccup. It was all very well for Eggingarde. She had got her story off her chest.

But Hiccup and his two little dragons lay awake in that darkness, listening to the sound of the Dragon Rebellion attacking the prison.

'You don't think that story was t-t-true, do you, Master?' whispered Toothless, his two eye-beams shining like torches in the darkness.

Oh, how Hiccup hoped not. 'I've never heard of a monster like that one,' Hiccup whispered back. 'Although there are said to be some weird things under the sands of the Amber Slavelands, things that have been cut off from the rest of the world for so long that they've developed in their own peculiar way, like Brainless Leg-Removers, Shooters and Slitherfangs. But I've never heard of a dragon with eyes on the ends of its claws...'

'So maybe it's not true...' said the Wodensfang, to Toothless's relief.

But although the little dragons eventually went to sleep, the Wodensfang's arms clasped rather sweetly around Toothless, protecting him, Hiccup could not sleep.

What if Eggingarde's story is true? thought Hiccup. *And what if it happened to Fishlegs? Please don't let it be true...*

Then Hiccup spoke sternly to himself. *Fishlegs is somewhere out there, and he is relying on me to stay hopeful.*

Hiccup was young and optimistic, and eventually he persuaded himself that Eggingarde's story was just a story, but a very good one, and he too fell asleep.

WHAT is under those sands?
Where is FISHLEGS?
Where is Fishlegs??
WHERE is Fishlegs????

Brainless Leg-Remover

~ STATISTICS ~

FEAR FACTOR: 5
ATTACK: 4
SPEED: 2
SIZE: 1
DISOBEDIENCE: 7

Brainless Leg-Removers are primitive
creatures that lurk beneath the sands of the
Amber Slavelands. Any sign of movement
on the sands above causes them to launch
upwards and snap shut their powerful
clam-like jaws, and then descend back
down into the depths of
the sands again.

8. HUNTING FOR THE AMBER IN THE AMBER SLAVELANDS

Very early the next morning, the slaves gathered in the prison courtyard for the Seeking.

Toothless was very tired and very scared, peering out of Hiccup's waistcoat. 'Toothless not want to go on this Seeking.'

Nor did Hiccup.

'OPEN THE DOORS TO THE AMBER SLAVELANDS!' cried Alvin the Treacherous.

C-CCREAK!

The great doors opened on the east side of the courtyard of Prison Darkheart and Hiccup got his first view of the sands of the Amber Slavelands.

It was the volcanic rock that had turned them that extraordinary bright scarlet red, like blood, and with the sinking of the tide they stretched out for miles, encircled by the arms of the Slaveland walls, as far as the eye could see and beyond.

'DIG FOR YOUR LIVES! HUNT TILL YOUR EYES DROP OUT! BUT TAKE CARE OF YOURSELVES FOR THOR'S SAKE... We've been losing a lot of slaves recently,' cried Alvin the Treacherous, and the cold clear note of the bugle rang out. 'THE SEEKING BEGINS!!!'

All around the edges of the courtyard, tucked away behind the crazy jumble of weaponry and dragon-traps, were rows and rows of sand-yachts. The crowds of slaves rushed and jostled for them now, for the witch's prize of freedom was far more precious than her punishment of death.

'Calmly, Amber-Hunters!' said Stoick the Vast, holding up his great hand. 'Calmly! There is plenty of time.'

So the Amber-Hunters got to the sand-yachts after the first undignified rush.

Eggingarde showed Hiccup his sand-yacht. 'This one hasn't got an owner,' said Eggingarde.

Hiccup swallowed.

'What happened to the *last* owner?' asked Hiccup, although he already knew the answer.

'I really can't say,' said Eggingarde, but her eyes seemed to say 'Lo-o-o-o-st...'

'Don't tell me, it's bad for morale,' Hiccup finished for her.

The sand-yacht was a wobbly, skew-whiff thing, with a basket balanced on one end to put the amber in, and a long pole, again slightly skew-whiff, to pole along the sand with.

In his mind Hiccup called this little yacht *The Hopeful Puffin 2*, because it reminded him so much of *The Hopeful Puffin*, the little boat he used to have on Berk, long ago. Before the war...

To give himself courage, and to remind him of that happy time he hoped would come again, he took out a piece of chalk from his rucksack, and drew a picture of *The Hopeful Puffin* on the side of the sand-yacht.

'You have to take care of your sand-yacht,' explained Eggingarde, 'because if your sand-yacht breaks a mast or something, there's no way you can get back to Prison Darkheart without the tide catching you.'

Every team had a prison guard. Alvin had put Snotlout in charge of the Amber-Hunters.

'But I'm a Chief and a dragon-fighter!' complained Snotlout furiously. 'I'm not a slave or a guard! I should be out there, beyond the prison walls, killing dragons for you, King. I'm way too important to this war effort for you to lose me on the sands.'

'Silence!' yelled Alvin. 'Are you disrespecting my orders, Chief Snotlout?'

Snotlout was silent. *He* was not

a fool. He knew what happened to people who disrespected Alvin's orders.

'Thank you,' purred Alvin. 'We've lost a lot of prison guards recently and we have to find that Jewel soon, my mother has seen it in her dreams, and Mother's dreams must be obeyed.'

So it was Snotlout who addressed the Amber-Hunters' party before they left. 'RIGHT, you 'orrible lot! You heard what Alvin said: hunt until your eyes drop out! And Stoick, Baggy and Gobber, please keep up. I don't want you old guys holding up the whole team,' he sneered.

So they followed the great army of yachts on to the sands.

Every now and then one little team ahead
of them broke off to begin working on one of the
pointless holes, or hunting for the amber, so as they
travelled farther and farther east across the sand, the
army of yachts grew smaller and smaller.

Until it was just the Amber-Hunters.

For hours and hours they sailed.

They had long left the islands and the land
behind.

The tide made a strange kind of sucking noise as
it sank, and it seemed as if it was bubbling, bursting,
and maybe it was Hiccup's imagination playing
tricks on him, but it seemed as if there really might
be something DOWN there, something that was
incubating, that the sands were about to give birth to
something dreadful...

There could be Brainless Leg-Removers down
there... There could be Rocket-Rages... There could
be something even worse than these...

The scary thing was that all the other slaves
seemed to think the same thing. They were very, very
jumpy, looking over their shoulders all the time.

Toothless and the Wodensfang peered anxiously
out of Hiccup's waistcoat.

'Do you think Eggingarde is right and there

is that Monster down there?' asked Toothless, querulously.

'Now, Toothless,' said the Wodensfang. 'If there *is* a Monster, we shall just have to try and reason with it. Us dragons are just as capable of evolving into more civilised beings as humans are...'

Yes, that was all very well, thought Hiccup, *but I would put a bet on that dragon not being very reasonable.*

Chief Snotlout found it hard to keep up with the Amber-Hunters.

The prison guards had wider, bigger sand-yachts and Snotlout hadn't yet mastered the rhythm of his.

Even Hiccup was faster than Snotlout, despite the fact the falling-apart *The Hopeful Puffin 2* was impossible to steer in a straight line, and wobbled its way forward in desperate zig-zags. (And in this it was very like *The Hopeful Puffin 1*, a valiant little boat, but it tended to go round in circles.)

'Stop! Slow down! Wait for me!' shouted Snotlout, waving his whip.

But nobody bothered waiting for Snotlout.

He fell further and further behind.

So when they finally reached the most evil of the Evil Reaches, way, way to the east, it was Stoick who addressed the Team with the customary Team Leader address.

'Ahem.' Stoick cleared his throat. 'Company of Amber-Hunters! We may be slaves, but we can still be the best slaves that we can be!'

Even the droopiest little Wanderer straightened his back at this.

'Present your kit for inspection!' ordered Stoick.

There was something heroic about the pathetic little line of yachts that arranged itself in a line out there on the desolate horror of the red sands, and the raggedy human backs ramrod-straight, presenting themselves proudly for inspection.

Stoick walked calmly up the line as if he were inspecting a war party back on Berk.

Snotlout came panting up.

'How dare you... puff puff...' He flapped his whip in an exhausted way. 'This is an outrage. *I'm* in charge here, not *you*, Stoick!

'We want to get as much amber as possible, you lazy slaves, so let's get you working as widely as we can,' puffed Snotlout, re-asserting his command.

'I'll stay here, where it's a bit safer, with a few of you as bodyguards, but the rest of you guys spread out as far as possible – *your* lives don't matter. Stoick, when we get back to the prison I shall put you on report.'

Snotlout pointed a shaking whip at Stoick.

And then something unexpected happened.

Gobber the Belch stepped forward and calmly wrestled Snotlout's whip from him, broke it in half, and gave it back to him.

'We are not in prison *now*, Snotlout,' said Gobber the Belch.

'Out here,' said Gobber the Belch, '*Stoick* is in charge.'

Crossing his arms, Gobber looked sternly down into Snotlout's eyes, as Snotlout swallowed, realising that these words might have a sinister significance.

It was true, they could not even *see* the prison out here, just the red sands that stretched out for

Out here, STOICK is in charge.

ever in all directions and the little group on their sand-yachts standing silently in the wilderness, many of them past their prime, but still old Warriors whose fighting ability Snotlout knew well.

And there were fifteen of *them* and only one of Snotlout.

'We have to go back sometime,' hissed Snotlout, shaking his broken whip. 'We cannot stay out here for ever. And when we do, I'll have you killed as a revolutionary...'

Gobber gave a dismissive snort, as if a fly was speaking, and turned to Stoick and gave the Hooligan salute.

'What are your orders, Chief Stoick the Vast?'

'Thank you, Warrior Gobber,' said Stoick the Vast, very dignified, straight-backed, every inch a Chief, the warrior he had been before he got the Slavemark. He saluted Gobber back.

Hiccup grinned in delight as the Amber-Hunters broke into applause, and Stoick bowed solemnly to them all. It was so lovely to see his father back in command, even if it was only temporary.

Stoick the Vast, O Hear His Name and Tremble once again, considered the situation.

It was much safer for all of them to stick together

in case You-Know-What attacked. (Stoick would not allow his mind to dwell on You-Know-What, whatever that was.)

But then perhaps it was worth taking a few risks because if they found the Jewel, they would win the ultimate prize. They would be free…

Stoick thought longingly of the idea of freedom.

Freedom. Dignity. Maybe perhaps he could be a Chief again? And then he'd never have to tell Valhallarama about this whole unfortunate episode. She didn't come home much after all. He could just hide the Slavemark under his helmet, like Hiccup used to do, and she'd never know anything about it…

Stoick closed his eyes and enjoyed this happy, unrealistic little fantasy, for one blissful moment. And then he opened his eyes again, and he was still there, on those blasted red sands, with the wind trying to blow him out of existence.

He looked up at the sun. 'It's a lovely bright day… Good visibility! OK, perhaps we should split into smaller groups. We'll cover twice as much territory that way. I'll be hunting with Eggingarde and… er… McBelly here,' announced Stoick, to Hiccup's surprise. 'Let's see if we can beat that streak of bad luck you've been having, eh, Eggingarde?'

Stoick gave Eggingarde a tired, encouraging smile.

Eggingarde pulled the hood of her bearsuit down so low she was a bit muffled. 'I'm not scared,' growled Eggingarde. 'That old Monster better be scared of me though, because us Wanderers are scary.

'Roarrr!' roared Eggingarde, making her fingers into claws.

Everybody pretended to be scared. 'Woah!' said Gobber, feigning falling over. 'Careful there Eggingarde, you nearly gave me a heart attack.'

What you could see of Eggingarde under the bearhood looked pleased.

'Has everybody got their whistles?'

Everybody nodded their heads. Around each neck was a whistle made out of an elk horn. 'You blow that as soon as you are in any kind of danger, and we'll all come and help you. Keep your eyes out for You-Know-What at all times and I'd say, we have, ooh,' Stoick squinted up at the sun, 'four hours before the tide comes in.

'Now, remember, if anyone finds the Jewel, other members of the team must stay together to protect the winner. And keep working closely in pairs so that if anything happens to your partner you can call for help.

If we find the Jewel, our prize will be the greatest prize of all, freedom itself!'

'Freedom!' cried the Company of Amber-Hunters lifting their nets on their long poles. 'We hunt for freedom!'

'Hang on a second,' spluttered Snotlout, as they all made ready their yachts. 'Aren't you even going to leave somebody with *me*? We all know there's *something* out here.' Snotlout's eyes flicked nervously over those endless scarlet sands. 'Something that takes the slaves... and MY life is too important to the Wilderwest to lose.'

MY - life is too important for the Wilderwest to lose...

'Oh you don't need somebody with you, Chief Snotlout,' grinned Gobber. 'You're far too tough. Nothing is going to want to eat YOU. You're too chewy.'

'I order you to stay here!' roared Snotlout, red in the face. 'I order you! Or I'll… I'll…'

'Or you'll what?' Gobber raised an eyebrow.

In answer, Snotlout turned his yacht around and sailed back as fast as he could in the direction of the prison. 'Or I'll report you for mutiny and treason!'

The older Warriors on the sands threw back their heads and laughed. Gobber let Snotlout get a little ahead. And then in a few leisurely strokes of his yacht he caught up with the furious, enraged Chief Snotlout of the Hooligan Tribe, sledging for all his worth out there in the middle of nowhere.

Gobber reached out a bear-like paw and flipped the yacht over, like he was flipping over a sea turtle.

DOWN tumbled Snotlout, somersaulting over and over. His yacht smashed, and he somersaulted over the top of it and got a mouth full of red sand.

'How dare you! You've broken my yacht!' spluttered Snotlout, spitting out sludgy red sand, and bits of little eels. YUCKY.

'I *have* broken your yacht,' said Gobber calmly. 'And now I'm going to break it some more.' With one big galumphing soldier step, he put his foot right through the bottom of it. SMASH.

Swoosh! Swoosh! Swoosh! All the other yachts came swooshing up and halted in a grinning ring around Snotlout, deliberately showering him in arcs of sand.

'Father!' said Snotlout desperately. 'Are you going to let them do this to me?'

'Am I your father?' said Baggybum grimly. Snotlout winced. 'I thought I was just Baggy, an old slave... Not really Chief material, I think you said...'

'I,' said Gobber the Belch, standing over the fallen Snotlout, with his hands on his hips, 'was once your teacher. And *you*, difficult as I find it now to believe, were once my star pupil.' Snotlout flinched.

'Talking of mutiny and treason, you yourself have betrayed most of the people standing here now on this sand. People who relied on you as their protector and leader. And so I am now about to become your teacher again. I hope you are not too old to teach. For I am going to teach you a lesson about being a Chief.'

Snotlout swallowed. He didn't think he was going to like this lesson.

'We are out here in the middle of nowhere,' said Gobber. 'Your yacht is broken. It is too far to walk back on foot. (That is why they gave us yachts in the first place.) You will be overtaken by the tide before you reach the prison.

'Your only hope,' said Gobber, 'is that one of us will save you by giving you a lift back on one of our yachts.'

The dreadful nature of his present situation began to dawn on Snotlout.

'We are about to leave you here alone,' said Gobber calmly. 'So you will have plenty of time to think. And what you should think about is this: what have I done as a Chief that will make someone here want to come back and save me?'

Silence. Absolute silence.

Snotlout looked up at a ring of cold, hard faces.

'Because,' said Gobber conversationally, 'it will have to be something good. That person will really have to *want* to save you. Your extra weight will slow down their yacht.

'Goodbye, Snotlout,' said Gobber. 'Think about it.'

All the yachts shot away. Leaving Snotlout alone, with his sword drawn, lying in the sand in the wreck of his broken yacht.

Thinking.

9. THE EVIL REACHES

So Hiccup and Stoick and Eggingarde set off to the east, and within a surprisingly short time they were on their own, the other members of the Amber-Hunters Team merely specks on the distant horizon.

Oooh dear...

Already this was really spooky.

No birds called over those sands. Not one. Why was that?

It must be because they sensed the danger that was below.

It was a horrible feeling, racing over those sands, because any minute Hiccup felt that something might reach out of them unexpectedly, and grab him by the ankle, like in Eggingarde's story.

Eggingarde didn't help his nerves either, because every time there was a perfectly harmless sucking noise, which was probably the draining of the tide or the 'glopping' of a scallop, she would roar at it, 'ROAR!', with a loudness and a suddenness that made you practically fall off your sand-yacht.

(It probably rather alarmed the scallop too.)

The hood of her bearsuit was so low down over her face that she couldn't see where she was going.

Hiccup would be sledging along and he'd suddenly realise Eggingarde had sailed off in the other direction so he'd have to go and collect her and put her back on course.

Eventually Stoick slowed down and started looking for amber.

Hiccup leaned out and scooped up something glinting in the sand, and then brought the net up to examine what it was. No, not amber at all, just a big old bit of crab shell. He threw it over his shoulder.

He sighed, looked warily around him at those bubbling sands to check there was nothing horrible rising out of them and moved forward. Half an hour passed, and he had found only three pieces of amber, all quite small, and none of them the Dragon Jewel.

He was suddenly bowed down by the hopeless ambition of what he was supposed to be doing. 'How am I, in this whole vast wilderness of sand, supposed to find one single Jewel?' whispered Hiccup.

'Your heart must be in your Quest,' said the Wodensfang, which was all very wise and supportive, but was actually *also*, to be honest, a little vague and not particularly helpful.

Hiccup sighed and carried on hunting.

It was quite an odd situation, to be out there on

the endless wilderness of the red sands with a father who doesn't realise you are his son.

'Go on, Hiccup,' whispered the Wodensfang encouragingly from inside Hiccup's waistcoat. 'Talk to your father. Tell him who you are, and why you are here. Tell him about your Quest...'

Tell your father who you are...

'It isn't so easy,' Hiccup whispered back.

He tried to push out of his mind the memory of Baggybum saying to Snotlout, 'I am ashamed to be your father.'

Stoick wouldn't say that, would he?

Perhaps he would, thought Hiccup. He felt slightly sick.

First I'll just try and get a sense of what he's thinking, Hiccup decided. *I'll just check that he's not too angry with me...*

Eggingarde was off at a little distance, roaring at scallops and picking up the amber with a pole nearly twice as long as she was. But Stoick was examining some amber a couple of feet away. Hiccup walked up behind him and said, as casually as he could, as if he were just interested in an off-hand sort of way, 'So, Chief Stoick, are you really the father of Hiccup Horrendous Haddock the Third, the boy the witch is searching the Wilderwest for?'

Stoick threw a piece of amber over his shoulder. He sailed on, checked the sands all around him to see that there was nothing alarming rising out of them, and Hiccup followed him.

'Why do you young people ask all these questions?' grumbled Stoick the Vast, putting out his net and scooping up amber, examining it, and throwing it over his shoulder again.

'OK!' gulped Hiccup, his voice sliding up from a gruff to a squeak, because it had been behaving in that uncontrolled manner quite a lot recently. 'I've changed

my mind!
You don't need
to answer my
question!'

But Stoick
seemed to need to
get something off his
chest.

'When I was young
I never asked questions,'
boomed Stoick. 'I just did
what I was told, I followed
the traditions, I stuck to the
Barbaric Code. I walked in the
path of my own father, and my
father's father, and my father's
father's father.'

For five minutes he worked in
silence, seeking the amber, grimly.

'I tried to bring up my son by the
same Code,' said Stoick. 'Even though he
was so different, and he always asked so
many questions.' Stoick sighed and shook
his head. 'But it is not always easy being a
parent. You do your best, of course…'

I know what he means, thought Hiccup, thinking of how hard it was training Toothless.

'So when my son asked the question, "Father, if you were King, would you free the dragons?" I told him the right answer. The only answer. The answer a King should give. Free the dragons? Nonsense! It strikes at our very livelihood, the world that we grew up in!'

Stoick shook his head, incredulously.

'But what does my son Hiccup do? He rejects my answer, beats his father in a swordfight! And goes over his father's head and asks for freedom for the dragons on his own!'

It's all my fault...
ALL MY FAULT...
ALL MY FAULT...

Is it going well?

Stoick was waving his arms around furiously, walking so fast, that Hiccup found it hard to keep up.

'And see what happens! The Archipelago is in flames around us! My honour, my reputation is gone, the ships I sailed in turned to ashes, my Chiefdom lost. All our villages burnt, the Dragon Furious rampant, the old order broken, the world at war.

'And all, all,' said Stoick firmly, coming to a stop, and looking deeply into Hiccup's eyes. '*All*... because of my son Hiccup and his questions.'

Silence.

'Can you blame me for being angry with my son?'

Hiccup did not say anything. He just walked forward miserably.

'Is it going well?' whispered the Wodensfang hopefully, because he couldn't quite hear through the wind and the waistcoat.

No. It wasn't going well.

His father blamed him for everything... His father would never forgive him... He was ashamed that Hiccup was his son...

ALL MY FAULT.

'And yet…' said Stoick, looking into the distance. And yet.

The pause that followed was very, very long.

'If you were to ask me *now*, the question, if I were King, would I free the dragons, I might answer you quite differently,' said Stoick at last. 'The experience of being a slave myself has strangely changed my mind.'

Stoick began to walk on, slowly. 'And now I ask myself… Was my son Hiccup actually *brave* to ask this question? Was he right to ask this question? Was it, even, a question worth losing a world for?

'So the answer to your question, McJelly, is yes, I am the father of Hiccup Horrendous Haddock the Third. I am hoping against hope that somewhere out there he is safe and well. And I am proud to be his father,' said Stoick the Vast. 'Even though I do not always agree with his questions, and I do not yet know whether they were worth the loss of the world I loved.'

It was the longest speech Stoick had ever made to Hiccup, and he did not even know that he was speaking to his son.

For the first time in a year, Hiccup's heart was lifting with a tiny glimmer of hope.

Is my father saying he might be able to forgive me? Is he even saying that he thought maybe I did the right thing?

How typical somehow, that Hiccup happened to be wearing an eye patch, an aromatic smell, and a large fake wart on the end of his nose for this most emotional moment.

Hiccup was about to say something... about to take off the eye patch, and the wart... about to say who he was... when two things happened that

interrupted him from doing it.

PPPAAAAARRPPPPPPP! came the very distant sound of a bugle.

'ROAR!' roared Eggingarde in surprise.

Up beyond the horizon where the Prison Darkheart was, one of those exploding Things rocketed into the air to tell them it was time to return before the tide came in.

At the same time, the sand crumbled below Hiccup's stationary sand-yacht, and the yacht tipped into an indentation in the sand.

Hiccup looked down, saw what it was, gave a start of horror, and said, 'Fa— I mean, Stoick the Vast! I think we should be making our way back to Darkheart, don't you?'

And he hurriedly picked up his yacht, and turned it around, and started sledging as fast as he could in the direction of the prison.

Thank Thor Toothless and Eggingarde hadn't seen that...

Stoick shielded his eyes, and looked out to where you could just see the shining glimmer of the tide on the horizon. 'We need to move fast now,' said Stoick.

They had plenty of amber, but no Dragon Jewel.

But they had to return to the prison, before

the tide came in.

Sailing as fast as they could, they met up with the other returning Amber-Hunters. All of them poled swiftly now, reaching astonishing speeds on those wet, sliding sands, afraid that they might yet be caught by that incoming tide.

They stopped only to pick up Snotface Snotlout, little though he deserved it.

We left Snotface Snotlout all alone on the Eastern Sands, do you remember? Thinking?

Well, he thought a great deal over the next two hours, and what he thought made him convinced that nobody was going to come back to save him.

He had been running back through that sludgy sand, though he knew that it was hopeless, and even running as fast as he could, he would never be able to out-run the incoming tide. Only a yacht could do that.

He was also attacked on the way by three Brainless Leg-Removers, and two smallish Rocket-Rages, which he had to fight off all on his own. So, all in all, when he finally saw the yachts returning to collect him he wept with relief.

Hiccup had never seen Snotlout cry: he wouldn't have believed it possible.

Baggybum and Gobber stopped on either side of

the weeping, exhausted boy.

'The lesson today,' said Gobber, 'was that you have done nothing to deserve us coming back to save you, Snotlout. Nothing at all. But we are going to save you nonetheless, because perhaps – just perhaps – you might do something in the future.'

Snotlout said nothing.

The two Warriors balanced Snotlout in between their two yachts, so that they could still go reasonably fast, and paddled back to the prison.

They did risk their lives for Snotlout, for he weighed down their yacht, and the rest of the slaves were already back at the prison, looking anxiously out at the incoming tide, worrying when they realised the Amber-Hunters were not back yet.

And then they spotted the Amber-Hunters on the horizon, racing against the tide, and cheered them, as one by one they reached the prison, moving so fast that they had difficulty stopping.

Gobber, Baggybum and Snotlout were the last in, so late that the tide caught under the yacht. The wave rolled in with the upended sled and carried them right up to the castle battlements, splashing against them with a wild swoosh...

And now, where there had been red sand as far as the eye could see, there was water instead.

Has Snotlout learnt his lesson yet?

We shall have to wait and see...

Snotlout did not speak to Alvin and the witch about the mutiny and treason as he had threatened to, and perhaps that was wise, because that unpleasant pair were not in the kind of mood to listen to complaints.

The witch and Alvin strolled up and down the bay with whips in their hands, examining each yacht returning from the Seeking, and shrieking with disappointment as each one did not contain the Dragon Jewel.

'Whereisitwhereisitwhereisit?' hissed the witch, bounding up to each and every yacht with greedy fury, and tumbling the contents out upon the sand when she found that they did not contain the Jewel.

'I do not understand it, Alvin. I saw it in my dream... The dice told me... I would be holding the Jewel in my hands within the next few days.

'YOU WILL GO TO THE EVIL REACHES AGAIN TOMORROW!' shrieked the witch. 'AND IF YOU DO NOT BRING ME THE JEWEL, DO NOT BOTHER COMING BACK!'

As Hiccup followed the slaves to the dungeon bedroom, he thought sadly of the ruins of his original plan. What was he going to do? Sneak in, rescue Fishlegs and his father, find the Jewel, and sneak out again.

This is going to be so much more difficult than I thought it was going to be.

He was trapped in the Amber Slavelands, and he had this terrible sinking feeling that he was never going to find the Jewel, or poor Fishlegs.

But all he could do was keep on looking, even though he was more scared than he had ever been before, now he knew what terrible dangers were lurking out here on the Amber Sands...

Because Hiccup did not tell Eggingarde and Stoick the Vast one small important detail. He didn't even tell the Wodensfang.

Back there, when the bugle rang out, and Eggingarde roared, his sand-yacht had tipped over. And he looked down and realised that the indentation in the sand was in fact... *the footprint of a gigantic dragon.*

And then when he looked up, he thought he just caught a glimpse of something out of the corner of his eye. Something so unlikely, that it seemed that it could not possibly exist.

The gigantic hand of a dragon sticking out of the sand, and on the end of each taloned finger, an evil dragon eye...

Watching… Waiting…

Hiccup had never seen anything quite like this dragon hand. It was absolutely horrible, like something out of a nightmare.

Hiccup did not tell Eggingarde because he thought it might be bad for morale.

10. THE DEADLY SHADOW

Hiccup was so tired he fell asleep immediately.

All around the castle battlements, the nightly shrieking and the screaming of the Dragon Rebellion had begun, the exploding weapons, the whine of the arrows being launched at the dragon attackers.

But while the sentries were on duty up there on the battlements, the rest of the prison was sleeping: witch, King, warriors, slaves and all.

And that night, through the quiet corridors of the sleeping prison, something moved like an invisible mist. You could not see the shining mirage of the Deadly Shadow as he crept through the rooms like a silent doom. But he was there nonetheless, like Death himself.

He knew exactly where he was heading.

Outside the dungeon entrance he paused, and his three heads sniffed with satisfaction, drinking in the smell of Hiccup.

If you could have seen the Shadow, you would have seen a gorgeous, shining invisible tail disappearing down the stairs going to the dungeon, like the tail of a beautiful imaginary cat entering a mouse hole.

But you couldn't see him.

Meanwhile, Hiccup woke up from a nightmare about the Monster of the Slavelands breaking into Prison Darkheart itself...

And then when he sat up, sweating, he found nothing there but the slaves all around him, sleeping the sleep of those who had spent an exhausting day sailing their way across the sands.

But what was that?

He thought he heard a noise, a noise that was nearer than the constant distant din of the Dragon Rebellion outside.

There it was again. He strained to hear the noise once more. Nothing.

Toothless and the Wodensfang were still snoring on the straw. They were sleeping so soundly. Surely that must mean it was nothing? Surely they would wake if there were any real danger?

But still Hiccup's heart beat as quick as a mouse. What was that noise? Was that the noise of nothing?

He was just thinking that the entire thing had been all in his imagination, when out of nowhere *something* jumped on him, wrapping itself tightly around his mouth so he could not scream, and he and the Wodensfang and Toothless were wrapped around

173

like a parcel and picked up off the bed.

The Wodensfang's ears were as purple as blueberries and jumping about pointing to north, south, east and west so violently they threatened to rattle themselves right off the poor Wodensfang's head.

'Danger!' the Wodensfang was trying to squeak. 'Danger! Danger! Danger!'

But Hiccup had already realised he was in a dangerous situation.

Hiccup tried to struggle but his arms and legs were clamped by his sides, as if by tentacles, or some strange invisible force so strong that he could barely move as he was inexorably carried off.

He was so scared he could hardly think. How could he be attacked from inside the castle? What could this be? His mind jostled with Rocket-Rages, with Piranha Hermit dragons, with Something Worse than all of these, something that could not possibly exist, a thing with a claw that had an eye atop every single talon.

But how could *any* of these things, in real life, sneak past the sentries that were currently blasting their way at anything that tried to get near the castle walls?

'Mff!' cried Hiccup, trying to kick out. 'Mff! Mff! Mff!'

11. A GENUINE SURPRISE

Hiccup could feel himself being carried up the dungeon stairs, could hear the sound of soft footsteps and whispers all around him, and then, as he struggled, he began to realise the voices he was hearing were not dragon voices, but human voices.

He had a feeling of being dragged into a smaller area, where the voices became more echoey and even colder than the dungeon. And then, more surprising still, he recognised the voice of someone he knew well, but just hadn't heard for a very long time...

'Don't panic,' said the voice. 'We're friends. We're here to help you escape from Prison Darkheart... We had to cover your mouth in case you screamed, because you weren't expecting us.'

And then the hands unwound him from the sheet he was wrapped in, and took the gag and blindfold from his head, and he was in what felt like some sort of drainage tunnel.

And he was surrounded by faces, the nearest of which he did, indeed, know very well.

'Camicazi!' whispered Hiccup in joyful surprise.

Camicazi was a small, chatty and recklessly brave Bog-Burglar, with a lot of wild blonde hair that looked like squirrels had been break-dancing vigorously in the back of it.

She also just so happened to be one of Hiccup's best friends.

Camicazi looked at him for a moment in puzzlement, and then she pulled up his eye patch, took off his wart, and exclaimed in gob-smacked happy astonishment, 'Hiccup!'

"Hiccup!"
exclaimed Camicazi

"Hiccup!"

Bog-Burglars aren't supposed to show when they're really pleased to see someone, so Camicazi now turned bright red with the effort of not knowing what to do. She scowled furiously, and pummelled Hiccup three times on the shoulder, and then she hugged him, and then she hit him again – a little harder this time – whispering ferociously (and if it hadn't been Camicazi, you might have said slightly tearfully), in between each punch.

'Where... have... you... *been*? I haven't been worried about you...' she added hastily. 'No, no, I haven't been worried, because us Bog-Burglars never worry, we're too cool, but where... have... you... *been*?'

'Ow!' grinned Hiccup, holding his slightly bruised shoulder. 'You're the first person who's actually recognised me. Not that I actually *want* people to recognise me in this place, but still, it's nice to know that I haven't changed completely in just a year.'

Camicazi was still bright red and scowling more furiously than ever. 'Why didn't you come and find me?' She hid her face in her elbow. 'Was it because I Turned My Back with everybody else when the witch got us to at the school? Because I'm sorry about that, Hiccup, and I've been wishing and wishing that I had

stood up for you, like
Fishlegs did, ever
since… It was just a
bit of a shock about
the Slavemark and
everything…'

'No, no,'
Hiccup assured
her. 'It wasn't that,
I knew all along that
you didn't really mean to
Turn Your Back.'

I'm so sorry
I turned my
back on you, Hiccup

'You're sure?' said
Camicazi, still a little muffled.

'Absolutely sure,' lied Hiccup awkwardly. 'Besides,
I was watching you the whole time and it wasn't
really a full turn, it was just a sort of twist… A kind
of sideways-on, Half-Turn if you like, and only for a
moment…'

'A Half-Turn?' sniffed Camicazi hopefully.

'The only reason I didn't come and find you was
that everybody's after me at the moment, and I didn't
want to put you in danger as well,' explained Hiccup.

'Well that wasn't very kind of you, was it?'
grinned Camicazi, who had cheered up no end.

178

'You know I *love* danger!' She rubbed her hands together excitedly. 'Danger is my favourite thing!'

Camicazi dressed as an Escape Artist →

DANGER is my favourite thing!

'Yes, well,' said Hiccup, changing the subject. 'Speaking of danger, what on earth are you doing here, Camicazi?'

'We're the Escape Artists,' explained Camicazi, beaming. 'This is my Team: Sporta… Typhoon… Harriettahorse… Beefburger…' She introduced the four Bog-Burglars who were sitting beside her in the drainage tunnel.

They had been the ones who had wrapped Hiccup in the sheet, and they must have carried him together along the corridor.

They were all considerably larger than Camicazi, but dressed similarly in black burglary suits, with a lot of burglary equipment and weaponry dangling off them.

To Hiccup's surprise, the other Bog-Burglars blushed and looked extremely self-conscious as they shook his hand. 'This isn't… *the Outcast*, is it?' blurted Typhoon.

Why, hello there, Toothless…

'That's right,' said Camicazi carelessly, but bursting with pride. 'This is *my friend*, the Outcast, Hiccup Horrendous Haddock the Third.'

It was very nice to have somebody being so proud to present him to others as their friend.

'Wow,' said Typhoon, pumping his hand. 'This is an honour. Camicazi's been telling us about your work, hasn't she, guys? Releasing the dragon-traps... standing up against those fiends Alvin and the witch... *Respect.*'

'Thank you,' said Hiccup, in surprise.

Meanwhile, Toothless was delighted too. Slinking behind Camicazi in the tunnel was Stormfly, Camicazi's gorgeous golden Mood-Dragon, who changed colour according to her mood, and Toothless was in love with Stormfly.

'H-h-hello, Stormfly,' stammered Toothless carelessly.

'Why hello there, Toothless,' said Stormfly.

'We're *O-o-outcasts*... You should see Toothless in an eye patch...'

'I bet you look marvellous...' simpered that mischievous Mood-Dragon, turning a little purple.

'And this is Toothless's side-kick... Er... W-w-wodensfang the Desperado. Don't cross him... He's one tough dragon...'

The Wodensfang was a little surprised to be introduced as Toothless's sidekick, but obligingly, he tried to make himself look tough, which was tricky for a dragon who was thousands of years old, no larger than a biscuit tin, and a little wobbly on his wings.

182

'There are p-p-posters up in the forest about us and everything,' boasted Toothless.

'Us Escape Artists are running an escape service, you see,' explained Camicazi. 'As soon as I heard that they'd taken Fishlegs to Darkheart, I put the team together. I thought, I've escaped from so many places *myself* over the years, why not go the whole hog and offer a truly professional escape service?

'Don't tell my mother, by the way…' added Camicazi, looking a bit guilty.

'You're a bit pongy, Hiccup,' she said conversationally. (Camicazi was always one to get straight to the point.)

'Stinkdragon,' explained Hiccup. 'It's part of my disguise.'

'Nice one!' admired Camicazi. 'Check out some of *mine*.'

She rifled in her rucksack, and brought out the Wilderwest Prison Guard costume, the dragon outfit ('In case we get cornered by a Dragon Rebellion attack'), the Peaceable Farmer get-up…

'They're fantastic, Camicazi,' said Hiccup. 'I think the moustache may go too far though…'

'No?' said Camicazi disappointed, and trying it on. 'It's one of my favourites.'

The peaceable Farmer outfit was one of Camicazi's less successful disguises...

'I'm just astonished that you've found a way out of this prison,' marvelled Hiccup. 'People have been trying to escape from here for centuries, not to mention the Dragon Furious has been trying to get in... it's amazing.'

Camicazi had a few faults, like most of us, one of which was that she was not very modest.

'That's because I'm brilliant,' said Camicazi, smugly. 'You have to look for a building's weaknesses, you see. Drainage tunnels, that sort of thing. Look at my collapsible ladder, made entirely out of broken oars!'

Oh dear, that ladder did look perhaps a little *too* collapsible.

'You can't beat a Bog-Burglar in a break-out situation, I'm telling you,' beamed Camicazi.

'And Fishlegs? Did you rescue Fishlegs?' Hiccup asked eagerly, his heart lifting with hope.

Camicazi shook her head sadly. 'No, we got here about a week ago and we were too late for Fishlegs.'

Oh no…

No, no, no, no, no…

'What do you think happened to him?' asked Hiccup.

Camicazi sighed. 'Well, when we arrived, we rescued this boy called Bobblehands,' she explained.

'Bug-eyed Bobblehands?' asked Hiccup.

Camicazi nodded. 'He showed us Fishlegs's bed, which is the one that you were sleeping in. He said that Fishlegs had gone missing the day before.'

Hiccup could not believe it.

Camicazi sighed. She knew what Hiccup was thinking. 'I know,' she said. '*I* didn't want to believe it either. Since then, even though we couldn't rescue Fishlegs, we've been trying to rescue a person every few days. Any more and we reckon the witch will start realising that something is up.'

Well, *that* explained why the people in the bed Hiccup had been sleeping in kept on mysteriously disappearing. Hiccup felt relieved on Eggingarde's behalf, because she must have been terrified when every morning she woke up and another one had gone. No wonder she thought that the Monster had taken them...

But what had happened to Fishlegs?

Hiccup touched the lobster necklace that Fishlegs had given him, for comfort.

As Camicazi had said, Fishlegs was the only one who had not Turned His Back at the Flashburn School of Swordfighting. Fishlegs had always been there, believing in Hiccup.

'I'm so glad we set up the escape service though!' said Camicazi. 'Now we can help *you* to escape!'

'I don't want to escape,' said Hiccup. 'I have to find Fishlegs.'

Camicazi looked very serious suddenly. 'Hiccup, you are the only chance we've got. The whole of the Archipelago is relying on you.'

'We are,' said Typhoon.

'You betcha,' said Harriettahorse.

'You have to face it, Hiccup,' said Camicazi, sadly. 'Fishlegs is gone. You should be out there finding the Jewel, and I don't think the Jewel is here.'

'Yes, we've all been thinking that, too,' said the Wodensfang. 'It's one of Grimbeard's red herrings...'

'What did the funny little brown dragon say?' asked Camicazi.

'Never mind,' said Hiccup stubbornly and defiantly. 'I'm not escaping... I'm still looking for Fishlegs, whatever you might say.'

Camicazi sighed. 'OK then, in which case I am staying here with you. You are only a boy, after all,' she reminded him condescendingly. 'You really need a girl to help protect you on this Quest.'

'You are not staying here,' argued Hiccup. 'What would your mother say?'

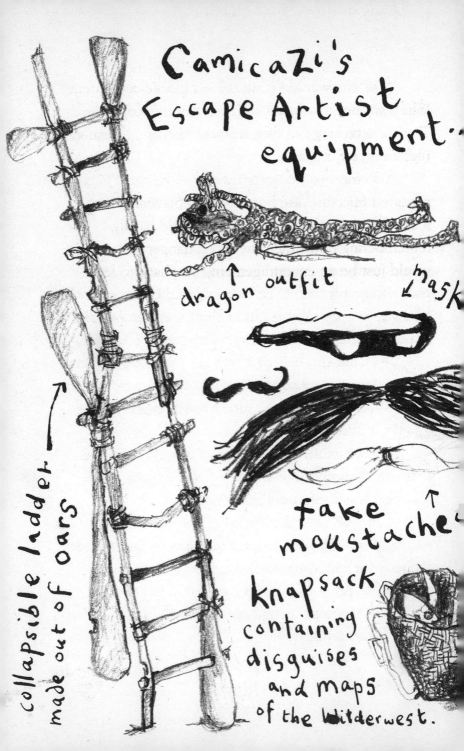

Camicazi's Escape Artist equipment...

← dragon outfit

mask ↓

fake moustache ↑

collapsible ladder made out of oars →

knapsack containing disguises and maps of the Wilderwest.

'Oh, she wouldn't mind,' lied Camicazi vaguely. 'She's got her hands full with the Dragon Rebellion. They're attacking the Bog-Burglar Islands every single night now, a bit like here...'

'No way are you staying here, Camicazi,' repeated Hiccup. 'You haven't got a Slavemark, it's way too dangerous. Besides,' he said hastily, remembering how much she loved danger and so this would just be an encouragement, 'you have to lead your escape service. There's this kid called Eggingarde who sleeps opposite me, and I think she really needs to escape, the whole Darkheart experience is getting her down.'

'All right, then!' said Camicazi, thoughtful for a second, and then allowing herself to be distracted. 'Bog-Burglars,' she addressed the Escape Artists in a loud conspiratorial whisper, 'lets put into action Operation Eggingarde!'

'Operation Eggingarde!' repeated Typhoon, Sporta, Harriettahorse and Beefburger, giving each other the Bog-Burglar high-five.

Fake Wilderwest
I.D. card ↘

The bearer
of this card,
Candyfloss the
Visithug, is a
loyal soldier of
the Wilderwest.

Grant them
safe conduct,

Signed:
King Alvin
the
redchero

12. BEAR-MAMA

Meanwhile the Deadly Shadow slunk through the door of the dungeon that Camicazi had left open.

You couldn't see it of course. But the *Sniff! Sniff! Sniff!*-ing noise went snuffling across the floor like the sludgy trail of an invisible snail, and a light wind blew through the centre of the dungeon.

The Deadly Shadow's talons were already out. Its broken heart was pure steel. The Red-Rage had so clouded its invisible eyes that they had almost become visible with hatred. The snuffling stopped at Hiccup's bed. The bed was empty. The Shadow gave a surprised snort and its talons raked through the remains of straw and bedding. Nothing there either. The boy must be somewhere else!

The Deadly Shadow was so steaming mad that for one moment he turned visible and you could see the actual smoke that was drifting out of all six of his ears.

The Shadow silently exploded what remained of the bed, and it stalked out the door again on furious silent tiptoes. And woe betide Hiccup if the creature ever found him...

Two minutes later, Hiccup and the Bog-Burglar

Escape Artists arrived back at the door of the dungeon.

'What has happened here?' whispered Hiccup, looking at his bed, which seemed, quite literally, to have exploded, sending a rain of straw all round it in every direction.

'Wow,' said Camicazi. 'You're a restless sleeper.'

Hiccup started trying to tidy it up. 'You'd better get a move on, guys, if you want to escape with Eggingarde before morning.'

So Camicazi and the Bog-Burglars were about to do their normal routine of bundling up Eggingarde in her blanket while she was still asleep, but Hiccup wouldn't let them. 'You might worry her,' said Hiccup.

So Hiccup woke her up gently.

'Ssh,' said Hiccup, 'these are some friends of mine, Eggingarde, and they're going to help you to escape back to your Tribe and your mother.'

Eggingarde looked at him with her big solemn eyes, and then she gave a huge, gap-toothed smile.

'Do you think I have a mother?' smiled Eggingarde.

Do you think I have a mother?

'I'm sure you do,' said Hiccup, 'and I bet she's been really missing you.' And he re-did the buttons on her bearsuit so they were in the right buttonholes, so she'd look her best for her mother.

'Camicazi?' whispered Hiccup. 'I think maybe you should deliver Eggingarde back to her Tribe, the Northern Wanderers. You'll find them up north somewhere, wandering about. Now that,' he added craftily, 'now *that* is going be a *really* dangerous mission, because you have to go through Dragon Rebellion Territory to get up there…'

'OK,' Camicazi whispered back.

Hiccup looked at her suspiciously.

It was unlike Camicazi to be quite so obedient.

'Byc then, Camicazi.'

'Bye,' said Camicazi, widening her big blue eyes innocently.

'Goodbye, Eggingarde,' whispered Hiccup.

'Goodbye, Hiccup,' Eggingarde whispered back.

'Goodbye, Stormfly,' said Toothless, doing three elaborate somersaults in the air to show off, nearly knocking himself out when he bumped into a pillar in the process, and then struggling to re-arrange himself in the air to look glamorous.

'Goodbye, Toothless the Outcast,' cooed the

Mood-Dragon, batting her eyelashes coquettishly at the slightly dazed Toothless as she followed Camicazi and the Bog-Burglar Escape Artists and Eggingarde tiptoeing out the room.

And that was how Eggingarde made her escape from the Amber Slavelands, and from this story, back to the safe warm arms of her mother, Bear-mama, (who had indeed been missing her), back to the magical stories of her scary Wanderer grandmother, and back to the admiration of her little brother Bearcub, whom she had never met.

OK, *so at least Camicazi is going to be all right and out of danger for a while,* thought Hiccup dozily. *It'll take the Bog-Burglar Escape Artists quite a long time to locate the Northern Wanderer Tribe.*

'I wonder who did this?' whispered the Wodensfang, looking at the rags and straw strewn all over the place, his ears doing that going-purple-and-indicating-danger thing.

'Wodensfang, you're paranoid,' said Hiccup, yawning.

'It's only paranoia,' whispered the Wodensfang, 'if things *aren't* out to get you...'

But Hiccup and Toothless were already asleep.

A Happy Ending for Eggingarde

Eggingarde
back in the arms
of Bear-mama

13. THE PAST HAS A WAY OF CATCHING UP WITH YOU

Very, very early the next morning, the first drizzle of sun rose over the Dragon's Graveyard. The Red-Rage attack subsided with the first appearance of the sun, and the Exploding Things fell silent on the battlements.

But who was this, picking his way in a little boat through the lingering smoke of the explosions, those grim cathedrals of dragons' bones where the seagulls are now shrieking?

It was the Hairy Scary Librarian, an old enemy of Hiccup's. He was a tall bent sinister figure, with a beard so long it was dribbling after him in the water like he was taking it for a swim, and two amber-nets on long poles that he called his 'Heart-Slicers'. The S on the Librarian's forehead proclaimed that he was a slave, but he was what was known as a 'trusty' slave, which meant that the prison guards trusted him to go out of the prison for short tasks and expeditions such as this one. He was collecting up the spears and ammunition so the Wilderwest Warriors could use them when the Rebellion attacked again tomorrow night.

The Hairy Scary Librarian poled his way past the dismal fresh corpse of a gigantic Rhinoback. He spotted something by a little island, hidden in the reeds. He stretched out his right-hand Heart-Slicer, and picked up the something in the net, and hauled it dripping wet into his boat.

It was a helmet.

The Hairy Scary Librarian tipped the helmet over, pouring out the water. 'Tick-tock' went the wheels in his brain, as he remembered the Visithug Warriors returning to the prison several weeks ago, saying how they had nearly caught Hiccup the Outcast, undoing dragon-traps again.

They had described Hiccup as wearing a very particular helmet. One, just like this one, with that rather stupid broken plume on the top.

'So-ho,' whispered the Hairy Scary Librarian, smiling a horrid smile. 'This is Hiccup's helmet, is it? Which meanssss,' smiled the Librarian, laughing wheezily to himself, 'that Hiccup is somewhere in the prison, and I can tell the witch, and get my own back on that horrible little Hiccup who is the reason I am here in the first place… and get my freedom into the bargain!'

The Librarian turned, and poled his way back to Prison Darkheart, slaloming crazily through the corpses, with all the eagerness of one who has waited long to settle an old score.

Everything we do, you see, has its consequences and repercussions, every kind act, and every bad, every friend we make, and every enemy.

Everything is connected.

14. THE LUCK TURNS ALVIN'S WAY

Horribly early the next morning, even earlier than normal, the prison guards woke everybody up by banging their swords on their shields and yelling: 'EVERYBODY UP AND IN THE COURTYARD! The witch Excellinor has called a crisis meeting!' Blearily and half-asleep, Hiccup staggered up the dungeon stairs to the courtyard with all the other slaves.

And then suddenly, he felt very awake indeed, nerve-tinglingly, eye-openingly, brilliantly awake, as he tried to peer between the enormous guy in front of him to see the witch and Alvin the Treacherous sitting at the table. The witch was tapping her iron fingernails...

... and in front of the witch was yet another someone who Hiccup knew from the past.

They say that the past has a way of catching up with you, and the distant and not-so-distant past was certainly catching up with Hiccup big-time, in the two days in which he had been trapped in the great Prison Darkheart.

The Hairy Scary Librarian was holding, in his

hands, Hiccup's helmet.

The one that Windwalker had accidentally left in the bay because he was so upset.

Aaargh.

It was too late for Hiccup to get away now. He was so wedged in by the crowd he couldn't even move.

Alvin the Treacherous stood up, his warts swelling with revolting gloating triumph like he'd just won the Barbaric Games.

'MISERABLE SLAVES OF THE AMBER SLAVELANDS!' called out Alvin. 'WE HAVE A TRAITOR IN OUR MIDST!'

Murmurs of astonishment among the slaves.

'This morning,' continued Alvin, 'one of our "trusty" slaves, Hairy here, was out in the bay of the Dragons' Graveyard cleaning up after the Dragon Rebellion attack, when he discovered this helmet.

'My Warriors tell me that this was the very helmet that was worn by that traitor Hiccup Horrendous Haddock the Third when they last found him undoing our dragon-traps.'

Oh for Thor's sake, thought Hiccup bitterly. *I knew I never liked that helmet.*

'And we have also recently discovered a secret door that opens on to a drainage tunnel that leads directly into the prison from outside…'

Hang on, thought Hiccup. *That wasn't me, it was the Bog-Burglar Escape Artists! They must have left the door open…*

'Which means,' said the witch silkily, 'that somehow that tricksy little Traitor of the Wilderwest has sneaked into this prison – the impostor – and he will be somewhere here among you slaves.'

Sensation in the courtyard, with everyone looking at one another, and wondering who the Traitor was.

'Of course,' purred the witch, 'we could get everyone to try on the helmet, and see who it fits…'

In which case I'll be fine, thought Hiccup, slightly hysterically, *because quite apart from being horribly itchy, that helmet never fitted.*

'But I,' smiled Alvin, 'have thought of a far neater plan. You see,' said Alvin, 'the reason that this Traitor-boy Hiccup can never be a King like me, is that to be a King you have to be strong and make tough decisions. Hiccup is weak,' sneered Alvin. 'He is too soft to be a King.

'HICCUP HORRENDOUS HADDOCK THE THIRD!' cried Alvin the Treacherous. 'GIVE YOURSELF UP, OR I SHALL KILL… THIS BOY.'

Alvin the Treacherous reached out with one arm and grabbed the nearest member of the Hooligan Tribe that he could see, and held his wicked hook to that boy's throat.

Now, the boy he grabbed happened to be Snotlout.

Alvin, you see, had forgotten that Hiccup and Snotlout were sworn enemies. He just knew that Hiccup was a member of the Hooligan Tribe and therefore would be sentimental about Hooligans and therefore grabbed the closest Hooligan he could find.

'Here I say,' objected Snotlout in astonishment, 'I'm not a slave, I'm a Warrior! And I'm your loyal subject, King Alvin. I was the one who told your mother about Hiccup having the Slavemark...'

Snotlout had already had a very difficult twenty-four hours. His ego had taken quite a bashing out there on the sands yesterday.

But you see, Alvin the Treacherous did not have a grateful nature.

Alvin ignored this, and if anything, held the hook

a little closer, so that blood dropped down from Snotlout's throat.

'YOU BETTER BE QUICK!' screamed Alvin. 'THIS HOOK IS HUNGRY!'

Now, this is what you might call a 'moral dilemma'.

Snotlout had been mean to Hiccup all his life.

He was a bully and a thoroughly bad lot. He was indeed the one who had thrown the stone that revealed Hiccup as having the Slavemark, when Hiccup had been about to be crowned Champion of Champions and King of the Wilderwest in the Flashburn School of Swordfighting.

But how could Hiccup, in cold blood, let Alvin the Treacherous kill Snotlout?

Snotlout was his cousin and a fellow human being.

And maybe, just maybe, very, very deep down indeed, there was some good in Snotlout after all. And possibly there was some way out of this completely packed courtyard, so he could escape even after he'd given himself up?

Hiccup sighed. *Maybe Alvin is right, maybe I am too weak to be a king... I can't believe I'm doing this for Snotlout of all people...*

And then he put up his hand and shouted:

'OK, I give myself up. I am Hiccup Horrendous Haddock the Third. I am the Outcast.' After a year on the run, it felt pretty scary to be finally revealing himself.

'Aha!' said Alvin in satisfaction, and he dropped a highly relieved Snotlout and looked out eagerly at the crowd of slaves. 'I knew it!' crowed Alvin.

Three rows back into the crowd, Stoick the Vast gasped in amazement, and tried to peer round to see where his son might be. 'Whiffy McSmelly! Surely… surely *you* cannot be Hiccup!'

'Yes,' Hiccup shouted up through the large people who were boxing him in. 'It is me!'

'But this is wonderful!' cried Stoick joyfully, jumping up and down, trying to look over people's heads. 'Hiccup! You're alive! I can't tell you how relieved I am, my boy… I… I… I'm so sorry I didn't recognise you… I can't believe I didn't recognise you…'

'Well, I *was* wearing my disguise,' Hiccup shouted back, to make him feel better. He took off his Really-Not-Very-Cunning-Disguise of the eye patch, and wiped off the remains of the dirt with the end of his sleeve. He couldn't remove the smell of course.

'And I changed a bit because I got a little older… I came to see if I could help…'

'Less talking!' yelled Alvin. 'Don't let the little rat talk, he's always talking his way out of trouble. Pass him up to the front, there!'

The crowd around Hiccup picked him up and, hand to hand, passed him over everyone's heads, up to the front where the witch and Alvin were standing.

'Ah yes, Hiccup,' said Stoick, trying not to breathe in as he passed over his head. 'You're looking well, but adolescence has hit you hard, my poor boy. The body odour can be bad in the teenage years…'

'Stinkdragon,' Hiccup explained, shaking his father's happy hand as he went by. 'So you wouldn't look at me too carefully.'

'Oh, that's a relief,' rattled Stoick, so off his balance that he did not know what he was saying, 'otherwise you'd have terrible trouble getting a girlfriend.

"HICCUP!"

But why are you here, Hiccup?'

The Visithug at the front of the crowd put Hiccup down gently in front of Alvin and the witch.

'I came to see if I could help,' said Hiccup. 'I came to see if I could rescue you.'

'Well done, Hiccup!' boomed Gobber, giving a supportive thumbs-up from the crowd. 'Very brave, coming here to rescue us!'

'Yes,' cried Stoick. 'Well done, son! I'm proud of you!'

'SHUDDUP!' screamed the witch. 'Rescue you? How could a little rat this small rescue you? Search him!' she screeched.

I came to rescue you...

'Uh-oh,' Toothless whispered to the Wodensfang, as the two little dragons crouched at the crack of Hiccup's waistcoat. 'We gotta go, W-w-wodensfang the Desperado... We're c-c-cornered...'

UH-oh, Wodensfang the Desperado, I think we're cornered...

'Fly!' whispered Hiccup in Dragonese, and the Wodensfang and Toothless burst out of Hiccup's waistcoat like twin humming-birds, Toothless giving out little bursts of fire, *pe-ow pe-ow pe-ow*, like he was trying to shoot his way out.

But the Hairy Scary Librarian was standing just next to Hiccup, and he was just as fast with his left hand as he was with his right. He drew those amber-nets from his belt quick as lightning, just as he used to draw his Heart-Slicer swords. (He used to use swords, but nets were his new thing.)

Flick flick, went the Hairy Scary Librarian's amber-nets, and he caught the Wodensfang with his left net and Toothless with his right, tied the ends of the nets up nice and tight and presented them to Alvin with a low cringing bow.

Toothless and the Wodensfang howled in horror, for dragons are wild creatures, and nothing upsets them more than being trapped.

And then the Librarian turned to Hiccup and narrowed his eyes. 'Never cross a Librarian,' spat the Hairy Scary Librarian with venom, his voice like broken glass. 'For Librarians are patient, and they can wait for their revenge...'

'Dragons!' screeched the witch triumphantly, pointing a dramatic finger at the Wodensfang and Toothless, all tangled and desperately struggling in the Librarian's amber-nets.

'I smell dragons, see! We are at war with the entire

Flick . Flick!

went the Librarian's Heart slicing amber nets...

dragon race, they have reduced our villages to black dust, and yet the Traitor carries *dragons* on him!'

The Warriors of the Wilderwest did not like that, under attack as they were every night by dragons, and they roared in fury.

'Don't worry, Mother!' said Alvin in delight. 'I'll just squash them with my foot!' He flung Toothless on the ground and lifted his metal foot.

'Noooooooo!' shrieked the witch. 'The toothless dragon is a Lost Thing, remember? We need him so you can be crowned King of the Wilderwest!'

'Curses!' swore Alvin the Treacherous. 'But I can still kill the other one!'

He flung the Wodensfang on the ground, all tangled still in the net.

'Noooooo!' shrieked Hiccup, thinking very speedily. 'I don't know which one is the Lost Thing, for they both have no teeth!'

(Quick as a wink, the Wodensfang sucked in his teeth.)

'Double curses!' swore Alvin the Treacherous, looking down at the supposedly-toothless Wodensfang in a baffled sort of way.

'But I can kill *something*, surely? I can kill Hiccup,' said Alvin, cheering up. 'Please, let me kill Hiccup, Mother. *He's* not a Lost Thing.'

'He's the *finder* of the King's Lost Things, though,' said the witch. 'Of course you can kill Hiccup, Alvin, my darling, and you'll do a lovely creative job of it, I know. But you'll just have to postpone that pleasure until he's found us the last Lost Thing, the Jewel...

HE is the finder of the King's Lost Things......

'The little rat draws the Lost Things to him like he's a little Lost-Thing *magnet*, rot him… We just have to motivate him properly, and luckily I am very good at motivating children.'

Ooh dear, shivered Hiccup, now completely petrified. *This doesn't sound too great…*

The Hairy Scary Librarian interrupted with an apologetic cough, cringing before the witch, and wiping his mouth with the end of his beard.

'Talking of motivation, I believe you offered freedom to any slave who brought you the little thieving magpie who is the Traitor of the Wilderwest. My Library is waiting for me, I've have been gone from it too long. Freedom, witch, freedom. I claim my freedom.' *Freedom*.

Again, it was pathetic to see how the crowds of slaves leaned forward eagerly. 'Freedom…' they crooned after the Librarian longingly. 'Freedom…'

Freedom to the Librarian meant being back in his Library, lurking through the passages, guarding his precious books, and in his mind he was already there, wandering the labyrinth, happy in that darkness.

But…

If there was anyone on this good green earth who was even less grateful than Alvin himself, it was

Alvin's mother Excellinor.

Now she had Hiccup to find her the Jewel, she no longer needed to motivate either the slaves or this Librarian.

'Freedom?' laughed the witch in surprise. 'What is this nonsense about freedom? Slaves can never be freed! The Slavemark is a Mark that can never be removed.'

'But,' sputtered the Librarian, 'you said it could be burnt off... You promised it could be burnt off...'

'I may have said a little white lie, but only because I care so much about winning this war for all of us,' lied the witch. 'Throw this Librarian back into the crowd!'

The Hairy Scary Librarian learnt the hard way, just *exactly* how empty is the promise of a witch.

'Now,' said the witch, bounding forward and crouching down to Hiccup's level. 'I am going to give you a very clear goal, Mister Clever-Clogs Lost-Thing Finder. I want you to find us the Dragon Jewel in... Oh...' The witch searched her mind for a good number and settled on three. 'In exactly three hours or I won't just kill the boy with the unfeasibly large nostrils, I'll kill everybody. I'll set the ticking-thing...'

Tick-tock, tick-tock.

'Three hours?' said Alvin in bewilderment, looking out through the open door at the end of the courtyard at the vast expanse of red sands, stretching out as far as the eye could see. 'You want him to find the Dragon Jewel in *three* hours? Um, Mother, these sands have been scoured by the amber-nets of thousands and thousands of slaves. If they haven't found the Jewel, how is Hiccup going to find it in just three hours? And Mother... there are those that think that maybe the Jewel is not here. Grimbeard had a terrible sense of humour, you know...' Alvin gestured to his hook. 'Look at my hand and the coffin-lid...'

'Hiccup is the Jewel-Finder!' shrieked the witch. 'He found the *Crown* of the Wilderwest in just three hours didn't he? When Flashburn had been looking for it for twenty years!

'Trust me, he's the kind of boy who needs a deadline.'

Oh for Thor's sake, she'd gone bananas.

'I wish you'd let me deal with him right now, instead,' grumbled Alvin. 'He's slipped through my hook so many times. Look what happened in the Flashburn School of Swordfighting, and in the forest of Berserk.'

'We won't make that mistake again,' said the witch. 'I've learnt my lesson. Last time I let him go down into the tunnels and the Fire Pit on his own. This time, we will not let the little rat out of our sight, for even one single second...

'Give the little horror the map!' screamed the witch. 'Get the little worm his sand-yacht! Get his nets! Get his poles! Put on his helmet—'

'I don't need the helmet,' Hiccup interrupted hastily, but the witch ignored him.

'Give the little nightmare all the equipment he needs!'

So the Warriors rushed around finding Hiccup his equipment, and kitting him out for the Seeking, and five minutes later Hiccup found himself standing on the slightly wobbly platform of *The Hopeful Puffin 2*, holding his amber-net in one shaking hand and Grimbeard the Ghastly's map of the Amber Slavelands in the other, and the horrible itchy helmet back, still not fitting, on his head.

Poor old Toothless and the Wodensfang, still in the Librarian's Heart-Slicer amber-nets, were now hanging from the end of the royal sand-boat, and they peered sadly through the nets at Hiccup.

And huddled around Hiccup in a circle was a

crowd of Warriors and slaves of the Wilderwest, hundreds and hundreds deep, all on their sand-yachts, all heavily armed with knives and swords and daggers, and axes and long-bows and clubs, and all of these weapons were pointed directly at Hiccup.

The witch wasn't taking any chances.

One big guy was even aiming one of those massive rocket launcher Thingummies at Hiccup. Not to mention a whole row of soldiers with their machines that threw five spears at once, and bows that launched twenty arrows simultaneously. Alvin alone could have overtaken Hiccup in three strokes of a heartbeat on his massive royal sand-yacht with the cutting edges, poled by Gumboil and at least three others, and he had screwed the Stormblade into his arm-attachment, just in case.

'Now...' hissed the witch. 'No sudden movements, you little reptile, or we'll blast you to Valhalla and back again... Show him, Gormless!'

Gormless let fly the spear-throwing machine, and *Ching! Ching! Ching! Ching! Ching! Ching!* Six spears buried themselves in a tight circle around *The Hopeful Puffin 2*. Hiccup gulped. 'One spear would kill me, witch,' said Hiccup. 'You don't need a hundred...'

'Find us the Jewel!' screamed Alvin the Treacherous.

15. HICCUP SETS OFF TO FIND THE JEWEL

Everyone was looking at Hiccup expectantly.

OK, *now* this really was a tricky situation.

He looked down at the map, hoping it would help, but he had looked at that map so many times in the last year, and it had never been helpful. The red herring Grimbeard had painted on the top somehow looked like it was laughing at him.

His visor fell down with a clang that sounded horribly like a death knell.

He edged *The Hopeful Puffin 2* out very slightly on to the endless red sands.

Hundreds of Warriors on their sand-yachts followed.

An outsider watching this would have seen it as ridiculous. Hiccup on his sand-yacht, *The Hopeful Puffin 2*, making its erratic way forward, followed by all these soldiers of the Wilderwest on their sand-yachts, all with their arrows pointing at Hiccup.

'Find it!' shrieked the witch. '*Now!*'

Hiccup moved the yacht forward a little.

And stopped.

Two hundred yachts followed a little.

And stopped.

'You're going to have to give me a little room,' Hiccup called out. 'To give my Jewel-finding-senses some space to develop.'

'Give the nasty toad a little room!' yelled the witch. 'But not too much room! Just a tiny bit of room! A little bit more! No, not that much!'

As if things weren't complicated enough, the basket on Hiccup's yacht was very, very heavy.

So heavy that it might have been filled with rocks and amber already.

And Hiccup suspected he knew why.

Those innocent blue eyes…

When Hiccup was a tiny bit ahead so no one would hear, he pulled up his visor (not without difficulty, the beastly thing still had a tendency to jam), and whispered softly out of the corner of his mouth, 'What are you doing in there, Camicazi? I told you to escape! And how did you know this was my sand-yacht?'

'You wrote *The Hopeful Puffin 2* on the back of it,' explained the basket, adding hastily, 'and I don't know what you're talking about. I've never heard of this Cami-whatsit.'

'Camicazi, I know perfectly well it's you in there,' hissed Hiccup. 'Why didn't you escape with the rest of your escape team?'

'I've trained the team well,' Camicazi whispered back. 'They can take the Eggingarde kid to the Wanderers without me. If you think I'm going to Half-Turn My Back on you again, Hiccup Horrendous Haddock the Third, you've got another think coming. From now on, I'm never letting you out of my sight. What's going on? It was very shrieky out there.'

'It's a long story,' said Hiccup. 'I have to find the

Jewel in three hours, or the witch will kill everybody.'

'But I'm not sure the Jewel is *out* here,' said Camicazi, in the basket.

'Try telling the witch that,' said Hiccup.

'So, do we attack?' said the basket after a while. 'I've got two drawn swords in here and a dagger between my teeth.'

'That may not be enough,' admitted Hiccup, looking at the hundreds of following sand-yachts, the thicket of swords, the rocket-launchers, the Warriors with their killer eyes all trained on *him*, the Northbows stretched to breaking-point.

'What's the plan, then?' asked Camicazi.

Hiccup sighed.

The truth was, at that particular moment he was all out of Plans.

The enormous wilderness of the sands-with-no- Jewel-in-them stretching in front of him, and the army of heavily armed people bristling with the worst in weaponry that the human mind could dream up, all edging threateningly up behind him, were slightly sapping his creativity.

He had that feeling of dread, again, sitting in his stomach like cold porridge.

'I'm not sure,' muttered Hiccup. 'Knowing that

dreadful trickster of a Grimbeard there is probably no Jewel for at least six miles in any direction. It's probably at the other end of the beastly Archipelago.'

'So you admit it!' said Camicazi delightedly.

'Steady... don't let the tricksy little rat out of your sight,' whispered the witch Excellinor from behind Hiccup and the sand-yacht. 'Keep your arrows steady now.

'Have you found it yet, you disgusting little shrimp?'

And then something truly extraordinary happened.

You have to see it through the witch's eyes, and the eyes of the hundreds and hundreds of slaves and Warriors of the Wilderwest gathered there on the sands.

To them, it must have seemed like some sort of miracle.

Some kind of supernatural magic.

There they were in their thousands, bristling with armour and with all their swords pointing at Hiccup, the guards with their sand-yachts with super-huge sails that could easily outrun Hiccup's battered old sand-yacht (particularly because he was weighed down by Camicazi, but of course, they didn't know that).

There was no way that Hiccup could possibly slip

through their fingers…

Absolutely no possible way.

But then one second he was in front of them, oaring his sand-yacht on its raggedy, slightly erratic progress, wobbling heavily to the left.

And the next, there was a rush of wind above their heads, a sort of blurring of the air as if a sudden very specific mist had come down…

And then there was a short, sharp cry and the next moment it was as if Hiccup, sand-yacht, basket and all, were swallowed up in one gulping swoop by the very air above them…

It was unbelievable.

One minute he was there, the next he was gone.

The crowd with their weapons and their axes and their swords looked at the spot where he was last seen with goggling eyes and jaws agape, and huge gasps of wondering, disbelieving, gob-smacked amazement.

'He's gone,' said Gumboil slowly. 'He's completely vanished…'

'NOOOOOO!!!!!!!!!!!' shrieked the witch. 'No! No! No! No! No!' as Gumboil hastily oared the witch's sand-yacht to the absolute spot where last he was. 'It's not possible! It's just not possible!'

King Alvin's royal sand-yacht came to a gloomy

swishing stop beside her. 'I did *tell* you, Mother. I have a long history with this brat, and we should have hooked him to death while we had a chance. I've been keeping my hook especially sharp on purpose.'

There is a kind of satisfaction that comes with being right, even when it is to your disadvantage. 'And now he even has the map...' said Alvin with a kind of grim, gloomy smugness.

'It's not possible!' screamed the witch. 'He must be here *somewhere*! DIG! DIG, you fools, DIG!'

The witch sprang animal-like from her sand-yacht, and began to dig herself, with her iron fingernails, raking up the sand in great handfuls like some desperate exasperated dog. As if, in some extraordinary way, Hiccup could have spirited himself below the sand, sand-yacht and all.

The Warriors and the slaves rushed to help her with their spades, digging yet another hopeless, pointless hole, like so many of the other hopeless pointless holes that they had dug in this bay.

Suddenly the witch paused in her hopeless digging, hands full of sand, and sniffed the air.

And she began to jump on all fours, and down to all fours again, like a cat leaping, and at the top of each leap she clawed the very air with her bony hands, as if she could scratch the boy out of the sky itself with her long, iron fingernails, and bring him down with her puny arms. 'He's up here! I know it! I know it! I can see it! With my true blind eyes I see him!' she screeched.

Quite an impressive effort for an elderly woman.

And the crowds of Warriors and curious slaves watching this on their sand-yachts began to whisper to each other: 'Ooh, she's lost it now. She was always on the edge, but now she's gone completely bananas...'

And then, because the Vikings are a superstitious lot, and impressed by anything that looks magic: 'Did you see the boy, though? Completely disappeared, into thin air...'

'I've heard he did the same thing a couple of years ago in the Fortress of Sinister. He flew, flew in the air, with no dragon, no anything...'

'No!'

'Absolutely, on my best blue helmet he did. Do you think he really could be the—'

'SILENCE!' roared Alvin the Treacherous, sensing the whispering. 'SILENCE. The next traitor that talks, they shall be talking to Hooky here, who is itching for blood as it is!'

Silence on the red sands.

'Half of you get down on your knees and dig!' howled Alvin the Treacherous, 'and the other half jump in the air for the boy in case he's still up there!'

Slowly the peoples of the Archipelago began to obey.

And if the great god Thor had been looking down

at that moment perhaps he might have reflected with an ironic smile at the state that the proud independent peoples of the Archipelago had got themselves into.

Hundreds upon hundreds of them, digging a pointless hole in the middle of the sands, or jumping fruitlessly in the air.

While the winds blew all around them and the sands stretched away for ever.

16. THE TRIPLE-HEADER DEADLY SHADOW

It was a very satisfactory moment to see the effect of Hiccup's magical disappearance on the witch and the crowds of the Wilderwest.

However, unfortunately, as you will have guessed, Hiccup's magical disappearance wasn't so very magical after all.

He had, in fact, been abducted by the Triple-Header Deadly Shadow dragon who was working as an assassin for the Dragon Furious.

The Wodensfang and Toothless guessed this of course, cowering and peering gloomily out of the nets swinging from the back of Alvin's royal sand-yacht.

'You see, I told him,' whispered the Wodensfang. 'I warned him about that dragon. It's only paranoia if things aren't out to get you... At least he's wearing his helmet...'

'At least he's earing his helmet...

'Yes,' said Toothless sadly. 'But what is he going to do without T-t-toothless to look after him? Hiccup *needs* Toothless... I'm one of the Lost Things... And I'm the best one...'

'Ooooooh!' squealed Camicazi from the basket. 'You *have* thought of a plan, I can feel it, I knew you would!'

Actually, Hiccup was just trying to work out what just happened.

They were in the claws of something that appeared to be invisible when Hiccup looked upwards, but Hiccup knew it must just be excellent camouflage. It could be a Stealth Dragon. Hiccup had come across those before.

And then with a very sick feeling, Hiccup remembered how the Wodensfang had been warning him for ages that they were being followed by something that the Dragon Furious had sent to kill him... How the bed last night had looked as if something had attacked it...

'This isn't a plan,' said Hiccup, in a petrified way, 'at least it may be a plan, but it isn't *my* plan, it's the Dragon Furious's plan.

'We've been abducted by some kind of camouflaged Stealth Dragon Thingummy that the

Dragon Furious must have sent to kill me.'

'Oh great!' sang Camicazi, popping up from the basket enthusiastically, like a wild blonde jack-in-the-box. 'I love Stealth Dragons!'

'So do I,' said Stormfly, emerging from the basket after Camicazi, and turning a beautiful flirtatious pale pink.

'I don't think
you're going to love *this* Stealth
Dragon,' Hiccup assured her
through chattering teeth.

Camicazi put up her finger.

'I'll get my emergency battle-axe then,' she said popping down into the basket. 'I brought it along just in case. And I've got a spare sword for you.' (Camicazi always came well-armed.) 'And then *you* can take one head, and I'll take *both* the others, because I'm the girl. You see, you did need me, I knew you would. Oh, this is exciting, it's just like old times!'

Hiccup didn't like to rain on Camicazi's parade, but there wasn't much chance of the two of them fighting it on their own.

He felt a little sick as he looked down over the invisible fist clutching the crushed sand-yacht, down, down at the red sands far below. Being abducted by a dragon, rather than flying it himself, always made his ears pop. He didn't know why, they weren't flying particularly high, but it was just one of those weird things. He took the sword that Camicazi was handing him in a shaking clammy hand.

Here we go, he thought.

The Deadly Shadow landed and held Hiccup and Camicazi and the crushed sand-yacht in one transparent claw. Above them the mighty beast towered.

'Let us go, you great see-through COWARD!' yelled Camicazi. 'Let us go so we can fight like

VIKINGS, you window-featured, triple-headed LIZARD-BRAIN!'

When it landed, the Deadly Shadow saw no need for disguise any more. The camouflage faded from its chameleon skin, and for the first time, Hiccup saw what species it was.

Uh-oh, they were in real trouble.

He'd never seen one of these before, but he knew this was a disaster.

It was a Deadly Shadow, and a Triple-Header at that, and Deadly Shadows shot lightning bolts as well as flame. It was a breathtaking sea-green when it wasn't camouflaged, and at least three metres tall and nine metres long. Way up in the six cheeks of its three heads you could see the faint bright yellow that told you that they contained poisonous ducts.

Like a creature this powerful really needs poison as well, thought Hiccup, slightly hysterically. *That's just overkill.*

'Wow,' breathed Stormfly, batting her naughty eyelashes at the Deadly Shadow. 'You ARE a magnificent creature, aren't you?'

Hiccup was trying to think of everything he knew about Deadly Shadows, but all he could think at that particular moment was:

Ooh dear, he looks cross.

WHOOF!

The Deadly Shadow leapt, and suddenly he was pinned to the ground, the breath being squeezed out of him. Hiccup and Camicazi gasped for air.

The creature opened its great jaws, and from all three of its heads there came a scream at so deep a pitch, and so loud, and coming from so many directions at once that the noise seemed to blow poor Hiccup's hair back and entered his entire being, and his whole skull rang with the noise as if it were being used as the clapper of a bell.

Hiccup and Camicazi may have passed out for a moment.

When Hiccup came to, the dragon's three jaws were stretched wide in front of him and Hiccup could see down in the depths of the throat of the one nearest to him, the muscles working, and he knew that this time the heads were going to shoot fire out of the fire-holes and this was going to be the end.

He would almost be relieved if it was, because at least it would be quick, and he wasn't sure if he could stand another blast of that roaring.

And just as he had closed his eyes and tensed for the final moment, one of the heads must have shouted 'STOP!'

Everything stopped.

Cautiously, Hiccup opened his eyes.

His head was still ringing.

Six green eyes looked down at him in a sort of stupefied amazement.

The dragon itself seemed to have gone rigid with shock.

And then the pink forked-tongue flicked out of the mouth of the nearest head.

Hiccup flinched, but it prickled downward, and sensitively, gently, it lifted the lobster-necklace that was hanging around Hiccup's neck, and the six eyes peered closer, closer, as if they could not believe what they were seeing.

The Red-Rage vanished from those six eyes, like the mist disappearing into nothing.

A great calmness and stillness came over the dragon standing over Hiccup, as he looked into Hiccup's eyes, as if the great three-headed animal was looking back through time.

One of the heads spoke, in a thrilling echo, so deep that it seemed to reverberate in Hiccup's heart. It was the unbearable longing with which it spoke that was so moving.

'He is wearing the lobster necklace...' said the middle head of the Deadly Shadow.

'He is...' hissed the others in reply, and all around Hiccup's head, they hissed like a nest of joyful serpents. 'He iss... He iss... He issssssssssss...'

... He is wearing lobster necklace...

... He isssss

He issssss ...

... He issss...

17. DID I ALREADY MENTION THAT THE PAST HAS A WAY OF CATCHING UP WITH THE PRESENT?

'It was a gift,' said Hiccup.

All three heads of the Deadly Shadow started in surprise, for it is unusual for a human to speak Dragonese.

And then the three heads spoke eagerly, again with that unbearable note in their voices, as if they had been longing for something for a very long time, and were thinking that the something they had long past hoped for was about to be snatched from them.

'So you are not the owner of this necklace? Who gave it to you? Where are they? Are they alive?'

The questions came from three directions at once, and delivered in those strange confusing voices it made Hiccup's head reel, as if the heads were speaking in some echoing confusing cave.

'He was my friend... He is alive... I hope he is alive... I am looking for him...' pleaded Hiccup. 'That is why I am here.'

Now the voices were stern, with an edge of menace.

'But you did not steal it? You are telling the truth? The boy who owned this necklace is alive?'

Hiccup swallowed.

'I really, really hope he is, because he is my best friend,' said Hiccup.

At that moment, Hiccup could see Fishlegs so clearly in his head, skinny Fishlegs with his sarcastic sense of humour and his glasses askew. For a moment it was as if he really was standing right there beside them, about to make some remark about the general all-round terrifying-ness of the Deadly Shadow himself.

'Look at us!' hissed the heads of the Deadly Shadow. 'Look at us! Look at us! Look at us!' The hissing was all around him. The three heads were whirring round him, confusing him, sliding back and forth and in and out of visibility... They were like a maze of mirrors... Where had he heard that phrase before?

Hiccup had trained himself to hold a dragon's gaze – no easy feat, for a dragon's gaze is hypnotic. If you hold it too long you find your will bending to theirs, or you are sick or pass out.

Certain dragons have a gaze that is almost like

a truth drug, it seems to drag the truth out of you, whether you want it to or not. And of course, triple the eyes, triple the strength.

Hiccup forced himself to look into the dragon's six great glistening eyes, which were now flecked with the reflection of the sky and it was like they were boring right into his head, into his very mind, and wandering around in the mazy passages in there.

And then there was a sucking sensation, as if they were dragging the thoughts out of him.

Not surprisingly, within seconds Hiccup felt dizzy, then sick – as you would if you had somebody wandering around inside your own brain – until he had to close his eyes before he passed out.

The dragon unclosed its fist of sky from around Hiccup's limp body, and from that of Camicazi. And the hand that was only minutes before squeezing the life out of them, and preparing to kill them, laid them gently, protectively on the sandy grass.

'What in the name of Thor and Woden and Freya's ickle pretty plaits is going on?' wondered Camicazi, trying to get her breath, holding her head and gazing at the Deadly Shadow in awe.

'I have abso-*lutely* no idea,' gasped Hiccup. 'But it's something to do with Fishlegs and this lobster necklace he gave me.

'But we're not safe yet...' he whispered. Hiccup knew this instinctively. 'The Deadly Shadow has not yet decided what to do with us.'

The Deadly Shadow strode around them, circling like an invisible tiger. Deep in its throats was a noise that in a less magnificent, noble, wild creature, might have been purring.

But that was not a happy purring, it was a purring that Hiccup knew well. That was a 'considering' purring. Toothless did exactly the same thing when he was trying to decide whether or not to do something.

Hiccup and Camicazi sat absolutely still in the sandy grass. Even Camicazi knew not to speak, and that their lives were in the balance. Round and round them the creature paced, the three heads arguing with one another. You couldn't see it, but you could hear it, feel it – the moving air, the great dragon footsteps all around them in the grass.

There were fifteen circles of great dragon footprints around them before the Deadly Shadow stopped circling and brought its three heads very close to Hiccup, the heads now visible and waving like snakes in front of a snake-charmer.

The middle head spoke.

'We have been at war with ourselves,' said the middle head in that doomy-echoey miasma of a voice.

Hiccup nodded his head respectfully.

'For there are two reasons why you are here. Two Quests. The first is as you say, you are looking for your friend, who you really believe is alive.' The first head gave what might have been a snarl, or a snort of appreciation, and sent a bolt of flame down into the sandy grass that made Hiccup and Camicazi jump.

'You spoke the truth,' said the middle head.

'But the Dragon Furious spoke the truth too. There is a second Quest...' said the middle head. 'You seek the Dragon Jewel. This is a dangerous Quest, and one that could have dreadful implications for the entire dragon race...

'For the Dragon Jewel is no ordinary Jewel. If it is found, it has a secret. And if a human knew that secret, he could use the power of the Jewel to kill not just one dragon, but *all* dragons. He could make us extinct, obliterate us for ever.

'But you seek it nonetheless...'

This time, the third head gave what was definitely a snarl – more than a snarl, a roar – and the bolt of flame that it sent out missed Hiccup by inches, and only because the middle head anticipated it and gave it a knock to the left.

'We have a dilemma ourselves,' said the middle head. 'For we have made two promises. One to the Dragon Furious, which was to kill you. The other to someone else, a long time ago. Innocence here, on my left,' (the left head bowed) 'would help you find this friend of yours, who means a great deal to us.

'On the other hand, Arrogance here' (the right head bowed and snarled) 'would kill you.

'I have the casting vote,' said the middle head.

It paused, and then continued slowly.

'Because the first promise that we made has a prior claim, we will help you.'

Hiccup gave a sigh of relief. The result really did seem to have been in the balance.

'Thank you,' said Hiccup, bowing his head. 'All I would say, is that there are others who seek the Jewel, and they would use it to destroy.'

'Ah,' said the middle head sadly, 'but they would never find it without your help.'

The Deadly Shadow knelt down beside them, inviting them to climb on its back.

'Come,' said the middle head compellingly. 'Take me to this friend of yours.'

Hiccup's stomach turned to jelly. Was it possible?
Here was a bewildering turn of events.

The dragon that was just trying to kill them, was
now trying to *help* them.

For one second Hiccup wondered if it could
be a trap, that the Deadly Shadow could be about
to take them to the Dragon Furious. But it could do
that anyway, without asking their permission, or saying
pretty please.

'What are you doing?' asked Camicazi, open-
mouthed, as Hiccup climbed aboard the shining
impossibility of the Deadly Shadow's back. 'That
dragon just tried to kill us!'

'It seems to have changed its minds,' said Hiccup.
'Are you coming?'

Nobody changed her mind quicker than
Camicazi.

'You betcha!' said Camicazi, thrusting both of her
swords and her emergency battle-axe in her belt. She
scrambled up after Hiccup and settled down behind
him, beaming all over her little monkey face. She gave
a sniff of satisfaction, and stroked the shining back. 'I
told you. I love Stealth Dragons.'

'Ooh so do I!' squealed Stormfly, turning a
passionate pink, and flying in and out of the three

heads in a flirtatious fashion.

'It's not a Stealth Dragon. It's a Deadly Shadow. By the way,' said Hiccup, addressing the middle head of the Deadly Shadow, 'if your brothers are called Innocence and Arrogance, what is your name?'

'Patience,' said the middle head. 'Because that's what I have to have.'

And the Deadly Shadow took off.

18. SEARCHING FOR FISHLEGS

At that moment, Hiccup didn't know why, but Eggingarde's story came into his head.

'Fly east,' Hiccup said, 'to the Evil Reaches... We are looking for a rock shaped like a witch's finger.'

The Deadly Shadow flew east. Hiccup did not want to find the rock shaped like a witch's finger, but he had to look.

One of those treacherous sea mists was

blowing in from the east, so the dragon had to swoop low over the red sands. For a long time he flew. Surely it was too long for anyone to yacht that far?

Looking down over the Deadly Shadow's shining shoulder, Hiccup saw what he dreaded to see.

A crooked jagged rock shaped like a witch's finger, pointing upwards to the sky… and a little way away was the speck of a yacht on the sand.

WE are LOOKING FOR a ROCK shaped like a witch's Finger…

'Down, Shadow! Down!' cried Hiccup in terror.

Down they flew, and as they grew closer, Hiccup could see, with a plummeting of his stomach, that the yacht was not upright. It was turned over, on its side.

Desperately, he looked to the horizon to the left, to the right, his eyes already blinking with tears. No sign of an untidy daddy-long-legs Fishlegs-figure anywhere.

Of course there could not be. Because suddenly the truth broke upon Hiccup, the truth that maybe he had known somewhere, all along.

The story that Eggingarde had told him, two nights before. That story about the Monster and the slave-boy? That story was not a story. It was true.

And the reason that Eggingarde would have known it to be true, was that *she was there...*

She was there. She was with Fishlegs when the Monster struck, and when that dreadful creature pulled Fishlegs beneath the sand.

It explained why she was so fearful, so scared of the Monster but not of anything else. Why she had told him the story as if she *had* to tell it, to get it off her chest.

It explained everything.

19. THE MONSTER AND THE SLAVE-BOY

The Deadly Shadow landed lightly on the sand.

Hiccup scrambled from his back and ran to the confused mess of belongings.

Maybe it wasn't Fishlegs…

Perhaps it was some other poor soul. It could have been ANYBODY, after all, they lost people to the Evil Reaches every day.

But when he reached the sand-yacht, Hiccup spotted something half-buried.

With a shaking hand, Hiccup drew it out.

The crushed, mangled remains of something.

The 'something' was Fishlegs's precious rucksack.

He had made that rucksack out of the lobster pot that he had been found in when he was a baby, and it contained the few belongings that he had owned in the world. Just to be absolutely certain, when Hiccup picked it up, a smashed bottle of Old Wrinkly's asthma potion fell out, and the potion leaked like blood staining into the sand.

Hiccup tried to re-shape the crushed, mangled remains of the lobster-pot-cum-rucksack back into its original shape.

This was it then. This meant that Fishlegs really was dead.

There was no hiding from it any more.

The Story of the Monster of the Amber Slavelands had been true after all.

It had been true and it had happened to Fishlegs.

Behind Hiccup crept the giant shining heads of the Deadly Shadow.

The poor animal seemed crushed. He had hoped against hope, and now those hopes had been crushed again.

The three heads sniffed the lobster pot.

'What was his name?' asked Patience.

'Fishlegs,' said Hiccup, crying.

'Fissssshlegsssss,' they hissed, waving like they were being snake-charmed again. 'Fissshlegsssss... Fissssshlegsssss... Fissshlegsssss...' they chanted performing a sad dance around the lobster-pot.

They seemed to recognise the lobster-pot, strangely, and they drank in the smell of it like it was the smell of the past. (There is nothing more evocative, nothing that brings back memories like smell.)

Hiccup held it up to the heads, unable to stop crying.

'I shouldn't have let him give me the lucky necklace,' sobbed Hiccup.

'I shouldn't have let him give away what little luck he had.'

'He may not be dead,' said the left head, Innocence, hopefully looking around. 'There are many islands around here. Maybe he got away. Perhaps he found one of the islands. Maybe he's still there...'

'Oh,' snorted Arrogance, 'you're deluded! Always looking on the bright side. He's clearly dead.'

At that, Hiccup felt overwhelmed. He sank down, crying, on the sand.

The Deadly Shadow cried too.

Even Camicazi and the Stormfly cried, and they *never* cried.

Hiccup could feel the wet sand below him, the red of the asthma potion that he had broken seeping into the front of his dragonskin fire-suit.

He cried until he was a little empty cried-out rag lying on the sand, the front of him now stained red.

A light rain was falling on him now. He could feel the sand below him getting a little wetter, as if the tide was going to rise.

GO BACK.

Something inside was speaking to him.

Go back and find the Jewel.

Become the King.

Do it for Fishlegs and everyone like him.

Defiantly, Hiccup dried his eyes with the edge of his sleeve.

He put the broken remains of Fishlegs' lobster-pot on his back, and staggered blindly towards the Deadly Shadow dragon.

Without a word, Camicazi was doing the same.

But then they stopped dead, for the Deadly Shadow was having an argument with itself again.

'If this Fissshlegssss is dead,' hissed Arrogance, 'then we no longer need keep our promise about the lobster-necklace.'

'But Fisshlegsss may not be dead!' said Innocence. (Neither Arrogance nor Patience looked very convinced by this argument.) 'And this boy is a friend of this Fisshlegsssss,' argued Innocence.

Patience was still undecided.

'The boy seeks the Jewel,' hissed Arrogance. 'And the Jewel must never fall into human hands...

'If we kill him, at least we keep our promise to the Dragon Furious, and the Jewel will be safe. For look, the human race is not capable of using such power wisely. In the end it can only destroy...'

Now Arrogance knew he had won the day.

The three heads narrowed their eyes and turned towards Hiccup.

'Uh-oh,' said Hiccup.

The three heads were lowered, dangerous.

Uh-oh, uh-oh, uh-oh.

The Deadly Shadow crept forward.

And fell to the ground with a shriek.

UH-OH,

20. OH DEAR

Oh dear, oh dear, oh dear, oh dear.

And that doesn't really cover it.

Oh dear, oh dear, oh dear, oh dear, oh DEAR.

You would have thought that you had heard the worst of it, wouldn't you, that Hiccup had had all that he could take. But, OH DEAR.

It's the little details we should not forget, the little things that catch us up, and trip us. The Warriors of the Wilderwest always set the dragon-traps in twos. so that if some other poor dragon landed beside to help another, then it would get caught too.

SNAP! The second trap snapped shut, catching the Deadly Shadow in its cruel jaws.

The Deadly Shadow put back its heads and howled the truly dreadful howl that a dragon howls when it is caught in a trap. It is an awful sound, for a dragon is a wild creature of the air, and so its horror of being trapped is such a ghastly wail of ultimate despair it is almost unbearable.

These howls were multiplied three times, and the dragon sent out great bolts of lightning all around it – north, south, east and west – with such randomness that Hiccup and Camicazi had to duck behind the sand-yacht. (Not that this would have been much good to them if the Deadly Shadow had scored a direct hit with a lightning bolt, but it's a sort of automatic reaction thing.)

The dragon howled and thrashed but it could not work its foot free.

Hiccup put his head above the edge of the sand-yacht and shouted, 'I can free your foot from the dragon-trap if you let me come near!'

And then ducked as a lightning bolt came singing over the top of his head, and there was a smell of burnt hair.

There was silence for a second, apart from the sound of the dragon heads arguing among themselves.

At last Patience called out, 'Come closse then...'

Hiccup stepped gingerly forward. The Deadly Shadow was lying on its side. It was trembling. Hiccup swallowed as he saw the trap.

It was immense and one of the most complicated he had ever seen, a fiendish contraption of clockwork complexity. It was far more complicated than it even needed to be to do its dreadful work, almost as if its maker had been showing off when he designed it.

Hiccup stroked the dragon's shining side soothingly.

'I can do this…' he said. 'I can do this…'
Thank Thor he had spent the last year
learning how to undo dragon-traps.
Hiccup took off his waistcoat and
knelt by the trap.

Camicazi drew both
swords, and started pacing
around the Deadly
Shadow, just as he had
paced around Hiccup
and Camicazi, earlier
in the day.

21. A STORY FROM THE PAST

The Deadly Shadow was lying very still.

The first head looked up, though, and spoke to Hiccup, who was working on that dragon-trap quicker than he had ever worked before.

'While we are waiting,' said Innocence, 'let me tell you the story of the necklace you wear around your neck. And then perhaps you can tell it to Fishlegs if you find him again.'

'He cannot find him again,' said Arrogance flatly. 'The Fishlegs boy is dead.'

'Let him tell the story,' said Patience longingly. 'Tell it... Tell it, Innocence. Tell it one last time... I want to remember.'

So Innocence began to speak.

Never had a story been told in stranger circumstances, the beautiful three-headed dragon caught in the trap, the red sands and the sense of danger all around. Hiccup working, working, to free the dragon.

But in fact the story had a kind of calming influence on Hiccup. It steadied his shivering hands – his hands that needed to be steady to unlock this trap.

The comforting, reverberating echo of Innocence's voice had a relaxing effect, like that of some sort of soothing drug. It was almost as if Innocence was telling the story somewhere safe, by some Viking fireside, and not in a moment of desperate peril, out on the red sands, deep in the territory of the Monster of the Amber Slavelands.

The Story of the Lobster Claw Necklace

'Not so long ago we had a human that belonged to us,' began Innocence.

'A human of our very own. Our mistress was a happy young girl,' continued Innocence. 'Half-Murderous, half-Berserk.'

'But you never would have guessed the Berserk bit,' Arrogance interrupted, getting suddenly into the mood of the story. 'She was so kind and gentle.'

'Her name was Termagant,' said Innocence. 'But it didn't suit her. She wasn't what you might call a natural Murderous, and she found the life of a Chieftain's daughter and her fiercely ambitious father, Chief Moody the Murderous, a bit difficult to handle, so she often used to escape from her father's village on my back, and we would come out here to explore the islands.

'This was our secret place.

'We were already a fully-grown riding-dragon when we met her, but with her we felt young again. Even Arrogance. She wasn't like all the other Murderous who beat their riding-dragons and kept them prisoner. Termagant was different. It seemed like she and us were the very same being, as if our wings were *her* wings, as if her heart were *our* heart.

'All was happy when she was growing up – but at that time we did not yet know of the human failing of falling in LOVE.

'Termagant fell in love with a poor wandering fisherman, very handsome, but not the Chieftain's Heir her father would have had her marry. Moody wanted sons of Chiefs with golden axes, not a poor fisherman, however handsome and loveable he was. Worse still, she married her fisherman, despite her father's anger. And worser still than all of that, the sea had its way, and one day her husband's fishing-boat went out in the middle of a storm and sank to the bottom of the ocean.'

'What is it with you humans and love?' growled Arrogance. 'It's a serious design flaw.'

'My mistress was so very very unhappy. Better to have never loved at all, than to shed the tears she shed. The only thing that kept her going was that she was carrying her husband's baby. She would lie, curled up on the windowsill of her father's house, with her head upon my flank, telling me what this dream baby would be like...

'He would be tall and handsome like her husband. He would be a poet like herself. He would be a Hero (of course), but not a boor like her father – he would be brave and fearless and yet kind to animals. Oh such dreams she had for that baby!

'But dreams and reality can be different, and most unfortunately when the baby was born, it turned out to be what the humans call a "runt".

'There's a saying that you humans have, what is it?'

'Only the strong can belong?' said Hiccup through white lips, fiddling with the locks on the dragon-trap. 'Throw out the freak or the Tribe will be weak? It kind of varies from Tribe to Tribe...'

'That's it,' said Innocence. 'I never will understand you humans.

'Well, Moody the Murderous was most hopping mad. He said it was a sign that Fate disapproved of her marriage.

'He told her he would have to put the baby in a lobster pot and set it out to sea, according to tradition, and the gods would see whether it lived or died. Mostly it died of course. It was very, very rare for a runt to survive to adulthood.

'Now, if Termagant had been stronger, she would have fought her father outright. But grief and the birth of the baby had made her weak. She made as if to obey him. But secretly she asked me to follow the lobster pot, once it had sailed out of sight of the beach and her father's stern eyes, and pick up the baby, and take it here to Hero's End.

' "I will come out and find you when I am strong enough. Will you make me a promise, Shadow?" said my mistress. "Promise that you will keep my baby safe until I can come and join him?"

'We could not make the human words.

'But we bowed our heads and bent down low in front of her to make the promise.

' "By our bright-green blood and shining claws, we will keep your baby safe," we whispered in Dragonese, as solemn a promise as a dragon can make.

'Termagant was weak, but she smiled, and stroked our heads. "I trust you absolutely," she said.

'Later that afternoon, she stood on the shore of the beach, poor Termagant, supported by her stern father, because she was so weak she could barely stand upright. All around her were the silent and solemn members of the Murderous Tribe.

'From around her own neck she took a necklace made out of a simple lobster claw.

'Around the baby's neck she placed the lobster-claw necklace, just like the one you have around your own neck. It was the very same lobster claw that the baby's father had given her as a love-gift on their marriage, for he could not afford gold or amber.

'The baby looked up at his mother with adoring eyes and smiled a shy smile.

'He tried to put his little hand up to his mouth with fragile, jerky movements, but he had to make a few attempts before he got it in the right place, and when he did he sucked thoughtfully on his knuckle.

'She stroked his cheek and kissed him again, drinking him in with her eyes as if she might be seeing him for the very last time.

' "Remember," she whispered.

'We listened hard, for what mothers say to their babies when they are about to be parted – well, that is worth listening to.

' "Hold on to this necklace and remember how much I love you, and that we will meet again one day, though destiny made us part. This is only a little absence, a temporary parting. I will come and find you, on the sweet island of Hero's End, and then we will be together for ever."

'She closed the baby's other little fist around the lobster necklace.

'And then with shaking hands, she wrapped the baby tight, and laid him in the lobster pot, tucking the blanket around him carefully so he wouldn't be cold, and she pushed the lobster pot out to sea.

'The Murderous lit their flares to honour the moment because it was sort of a funeral, although the baby was still living. And as was traditional, they fired burning arrows that landed harmlessly on either side of the baby's little craft as it drifted gently out to sea, and the baby took his knuckle out of his mouth and made a gurgle of delight, reaching out his arms as if he thought he could touch the beautiful flaming arrows as they rained down all around him.

'He did not know this was supposed to be his funeral, but looked about him expectantly – at the beautiful blue sky above, at the bright and interesting world that awaited him, the slow arcs of seagulls flying way, way up high overhead, until the very, very gentle rocking of the pillows of the waves below him, made his eyes... slowly... close, and lulled him into sleep.

'The Murderous Tribe were proud, sad and solemn on the beach. Termagant was crying hard, and as the little lobster pot crept further and further out to sea on the back of each gentle wave, she staggered up the beach back to the Murderous village, supported by the arm of her proud unbending father. The Murderous Tribe followed.

'We had been sitting there all this time, a great camouflaged statue, noticed by none, lying at the back of the beach.

'Now was our moment. We leapt into the air, over the heads of the departing crowd, invisible to their eyes, although a few may have looked up as the breeze from our wings caught the hairs on the back of their necks.

'Termagant looked up. We saw her look up, and she smiled through her tears, and she stood straight up – though it was hard for her, she was so weak – and made the Viking salute, and cried out, "Remember! We'll meet again!"

'Moody looked up too, surprised, but all HE saw was the clouds and the winds and the screaming seagulls. Over their heads we flew, off towards the little speck of the baby, far out to sea now and only a tiny speck on the horizon.

'We can still see the sea, now,' said Innocence.

'I can see it,' said Patience, looking back into the past. 'I remember it like it was yesterday.'

'Me too,' said Arrogance.

'Flat as glass it was,' said Innocence, 'and the baby was quietly sleeping in his little lobster-boat, drifting eastwards. Nearer, nearer we got with our quiet, ghost wings, flying high over the bay. Our dragon eyes are as acute as our dragon ears. Nobody's senses are more acute than a Deadly Shadow's. We were still far away but we could see, way down below us, that there was not even a lap of water coming over the edge to wet the blanket that wrapped him. He was sleeping so peacefully, with his little fist still clutched trustingly around the lobster necklace.

'It was a summer's day. But even summer's days in the Archipelago can be changeable, and as we came out of the shelter of the bay, out of nowhere it seemed, the treacherous Archipelago wind blew in a southern storm and a thick smoky sea-mist so dense it was like a white blindfold. In a couple of flaps of our wings, we had lost sight of the baby...

'We lost sight of everything...

'Even OUR dragon eyes cannot see through mist. They cannot hear a sleeping baby.'

Both Patience and Arrogance groaned at the memory.

'We panicked – the baby! The baby! We screeched in alarm, trying to wake the baby up so at least we could hear him crying. But the baby did not wake up. We flew desperately from left to right, but it was no use, we did not know west from east or east from west. For an hour we flapped, so disorientated, so panicked and terrified, that we plunged from time to time into the ice cold sea... And when the mist rose, when the mist rose...

'... the baby was gone.'

There was an awful silence.

'We looked for the baby for the next two weeks,' whispered Innocence. 'We searched every cove, every possible beach where the wind might have carried him to safety. And then, one dreadful day, we found the blue and white blanket floating in a bay far, far to the east. We took it as a sign that poor Termagant's baby had gone to the bottom of the sea, like his father before him.'

'What happened to the mother?' asked Hiccup.

The three heads sighed a sigh of infinite sadness. 'We crept back to see her. We did not want to go. Just one sight of us, and she would have known the terrible news. But she had not made it through her illness. She had already died. But at least she died believing that her baby was safe with us on Hero's End, and that would have made her happy.'

'Termagant died?'

'Our grief was so terrible,' said Arrogance. 'It was as if the sun had gone away.'

'So what happened to you after that?' asked Hiccup.

'We could not go back to Hero's End,' said Patience. 'We felt so guilty. She trusted us absolutely, and we had broken our promise. We flew up into the Murderous Mountains where we had spent our childhood, and we tried to forget her. We tried to forget everything and live our life as a wild dragon again. Fourteen years is a long time... We began to forget, and then we heard the call of the Red-Rage and joined the Dragon Rebellion. THAT helped the forgetting all right. It was only when we saw the lobster necklace again, around your neck, that we remembered...'

Not Quite
THE END
of the Story

22. WHAT HAPPENED NEXT

There was a pause on the red sands as the dragons finished telling their tale.

'Well, I will tell you,' said Hiccup, 'what happened to the baby after you lost sight of him. He was washed up on Long Beach, and the Tribe built a hut for him to live in. A Long-Eared Caretaker Dragon looked after him, and he turned out to be my best friend, Fishlegs.'

'You see?' said Innocence. 'I always said how he must have survived, and you two never believed me.'

The three heads sighed.

'I have to say,' admitted Arrogance, 'I never dreamed that there could have been a happy end to *that* story.'

'There's always hope,' said Innocence.

The Deadly Shadow's three heads were lying on the sand, looking back into the past.

And then, quite suddenly, Hiccup thought that the sand below his knees was feeling just a little wetter than it had before. He looked at the horizon. The tide was coming in…

Patience put down his head and nudged Hiccup's head upwards so that he looked at him. He put one paw on one side of Hiccup's head and looked straight into Hiccup's eyes. They were so close, that you could just see the vague outline of the irises, the black of the pupils. Kind eyes.

'I think perhaps, you should leave us now,' Patience said casually. 'The Monster is coming, and the tide will come in, and so this is your last chance to go back on the sand-yacht. The Monster will not eat dragon-flesh. We are too tough for it.'

How strange dragons are, thought Hiccup. *This one can move from cruelty to selfless kindness in a heartbeat.*

'Leave us,' said Patience.

'Leave usss,' repeated Innocence and Arrogance.

'We won't drown,' Patience assured him. 'We have gills.'

Hiccup dropped his head from the mesmerising, hypnotising gaze and carried on working at the dragon-trap. 'You lie. You're not a Sea Dragon,' said Hiccup shortly. Trust Hiccup to know his dragon species. 'You're an Air Dragon. Those gills only work up to a certain point.'

But after a minute he called out to Camicazi, who was patrolling around them with her fiercest Bog-Burglar expression, two swords drawn.

'Camicazi,' he said as casually as he could,

'maybe you ought to go back on that sand-yacht and fetch help.'

'What kind of an idiot do you take me for?' Camicazi yelled back, extremely affronted. 'I'm not a five-year-old! And I'm not leaving until you're leaving.'

Hiccup worked on, shivering now, in the cold wind, fingers numb, his dragon-suit pathetically stained with red.

On, on, Hiccup worked.

Ten minutes had passed. The sand was definitely wetter now, the sea on the horizon was gleamingly near.

Fifteen minutes gone...

But he was so close now, he could feel it, so close...

And oh joy!

The pieces of the locks fell apart in his hands, and the trap sprang open.

It is such a wonderful moment when that happens.

'Just in time,' Hiccup gasped.

The Deadly Shadow let out three roars of triumph, beat his mighty wings and launched into the air and hovered there.

He reached out to pick up Hiccup off the sand.

Hiccup reached out his own hands towards the

now airborne dragon, and he felt a horrible clammy
something grab him with dreadful force around the
ankle...

'Hiccup!!!!!' screamed Camicazi...

... as a gigantic dragon claw, with huge eyes on
the end of it, dragged Hiccup down, down, down,
below the sand.

23. SOME DRAGONS REALLY ARE MONSTERS

If you or I had felt a claw creep around our ankles in such a situation, we would have screamed.

But Hiccup had been in so many terrifying and dangerous adventures in his short life that he did not scream, for he knew he did not have time. He took a great breath of air instead, and held his nose, as the unknown creature dragged him downwards through the sand.

DOWN, DOWN, DOWN!

Just as Hiccup thought he was going to pass out, the creature pulling him below seemed to break through some sort of wall, and Hiccup landed with a bone-crunching jolt on something hard and his hand flew off his nose and he took a great involuntary breath...

... not of sand, but of air – rancid, stuffy dank air that caught in the throat like slug breath. And he coughed and gasped, sand pouring out of his ears and from his hair.

As he tried to open his eyes, gritty with grains of sand, he could see blurrily through streaming tears, sand still pouring down from a hole.

But the Monster with the eye-claws was shooting flames upward in continuous bursts of hot, then freezing, flame. This turned the sand pouring through into something that looked like glass, sealing the hole.

They seemed to be in some sort of cavern, and the Monster moved its head this way and that, reinforcing the glass walls of the tunnel.

The flames stopped.

Hiccup could hear the Wodensfang's little quavery voice in his head, 'Now, now, Hiccup, dragons are not Monsters you know...'

But the thing is, just as some humans can be evil, some dragons really *are* Monsters.

You should never judge a book by its cover, but on this occasion, Hiccup felt he was on fairly safe ground. This Monster's primitive and ghastly appearance told him there would be no point reasoning with it (however optimistic the Wodensfang might be about the possibility of dragons evolving consciences and complicated things like that).

This Monster couldn't evolve a conscience in the next thirty seconds, and it was unlikely to be a sympathetic audience.

There is such a huge variety of dragon species, you see.

Some dragons, Sea Dragons like the Wodensfang, have copied humans to such a large extent that they can use language fluently. They are able to reason, to think.

Others that Hiccup had come across like Darkbreathers, and Monstrous Strangulators, are not capable of complicated thinking processes. These are dragons that have spent most of their lives underground or in the depths of the ocean. All that time alone in the dark does not help the development of an appreciation for the finer things in life.

A year of living on his wits had sharpened Hiccup's ability to weigh up deadly situations like this in an instant.

He couldn't reason with this dragon. So he would have to fight it. He thought fast – very fast – as he scanned his enemy.

Fifteen feet of well-armed muscled dragon.

Burrowing Slitherfangs

Slitherfangs live under the sand a pull victims under the sand wit tentackles.

1. Slitherfangs swallow prey without biting

Ten eyes. Huge claws. An interesting snakey aspect that suggested it might be related to a Slitherfang, which also lived under the sand.

Quickly glancing the other way, he assessed his chances of escape.

The cavern was bare with only one immediate escape route.

And judging from the bulging leg muscles, the Monster would reach it first.

This was a tricky situation.

His only chance was to hope that this creature really was a primitive relation of a Slitherfang, and to use his knowledge of Slitherfangs to fight it.

Racking his brain, Hiccup tried to remember everything he could about Slitherfangs. What did he know? What had he written about them in his notebooks?

I HATE SNOTLOUT

Nad

tentakles

5. Slitherfangs have a small, vulnerable spot on their foreheads.

6. Slitherfangs like to swallow their prey hole while still warm BUT dont let them!!!

The Monster had a small weak spot right in the middle of its forehead. There was only one way he could reach that small vulnerable spot, given that the Monster was so heavily armed with talons and teeth.

If he could get the creature to believe that he was dead, it would want to swallow him immediately.

He would then have to allow the creature to swallow him whole and look for the opportunity to attack the creature's only vulnerable spot.

He'd have to be patient. He'd have to let the Monster swallow him at least up to the knees, so that it would be harder for it to react when Hiccup reached down and plunged his sword into the weak spot.

Thank Thor he had a sword on him, or rather, thank Camicazi. If she hadn't stowed away in his sand-yacht and given him her spare sword, he wouldn't even be able to carry out *this* totally desperate and ridiculous plan.

The success of Hiccup's plan depended on one crucial point. The creature would have to swallow him from the *right end*, that is, starting with his feet. There wasn't a lot he could do if it started swallowing his *head*.

This was a fifty-fifty chance, which isn't normally

a good proposition when your life depends on it, but sometimes you just have to give yourself up to the fickle hand of Fate, the toss of a coin.

It wasn't very hard for Hiccup to pretend to be dead, frankly, for he very nearly WAS dead.

He made himself go limp, even though every nerve in his body was screaming at him to run away. He forced his body to go limper and limper, and his head to loll backwards.

He kept his eyes open, just the tiniest, smidgiest of cracks so that he could see what was going on.

He forced himself to lie still as he felt something yucky slide up over his body. It took all of his powers of concentration to stop himself from moving, from jumping up, from shaking off the sand that was gritting all over his body and that disgusting dragon hand that he could see through the cracks of his eyelids.

He had to stop himself from crying out in horror at the sight of the two monstrous claws – five fingers, each with an evil dragon eye perched on the end just above the talons. The dragon's face was blind, with two ghostly hollows where its eyes should have been. But the ten dragon eyes were blinking down at him from the end of the creature's claws.

BLINK BLINK.

They were shark's eyes, dead.

The creature felt its way along Hiccup's body. Its long tail had wrapped its way round Hiccup's torso and was squeezing the life out of him.

Maybe I **AM** *dead, after all*, he thought semi-dreamily, and it was almost as if his spirit left his body for a moment to look down on his own unconscious body as it lay strangled by the horrible Monster in the glass maze, squeezing, squeezing.

All twenty eyes stopped at Hiccup's chest area.

You have to remember, that when Hiccup had prostrated himself on the sand earlier on, he had soaked himself in the broken bottle of Old Wrinkly's Asthma Potion, and that potion was a deep crimson red colour, exactly the colour of human blood.

So he really looked a very limp and gory sight indeed, covered from top to toe, but particularly on his front, in lashings and lashings of bright red blood. The Monster gently wiped the sand off him, and even the Monster knew that humans could not lose this much blood and live.

'He's dead...' mused the Monster to itself, very disappointed. 'He won't squeak for me, however hard I squeeze. And dead men start to smell...'

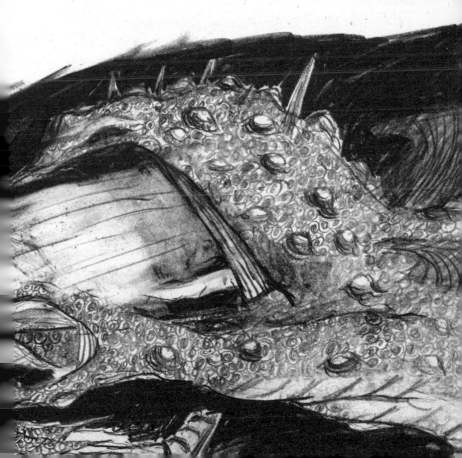

Like many underground creatures, Slitherfangs like to keep a tidy burrow, and dead things do indeed smell, a smell that is magnified if one is buried suffocatingly some way underground.

'I'll have to EAT it right now and here,' the Monster decided.

So the *first* part of Hiccup's plan was a success, at least.

Although it might seem to be a strange sort of success.

The Monster thought he was dead, and had decided to eat him.

The Monster, who was a picky eater, blasted Hiccup with sea-water to get off all the sand ('Too gritty'), rolling him over and over. And then the Monster began to coat him with some revolting greasy substance to make him go down the easier.

Aha, thought Hiccup, with infinite relief. *I was right, it is like a Slitherfang. It wants to swallow me whole.* That was a weight off his mind, because it would mean there would be no teeth involved in the process, no chewing.

And then the Monster picked up Hiccup by one leg, and blasted the ground underneath him with fire and sea-water to make a nice clean glass surface to eat off, because like Slitherfangs, it seemed to be very pernickety about such things, and laid him down carefully, arranging his arms by his sides.

Then there was a pause, during which Hiccup was absolutely dying to open his eyes, and a horrible, horrible moment when he could feel the Monster sniffing, sniffing at his ears...

It's going to start at the wrong end! thought Hiccup, desperately trying to think of a plan on the spur of the moment that would work on killing a dragon that was swallowing your head.

But just as he was about to do something stupid like try and jump to his feet, he felt a sort of snuffling on his right big toe.

The Monster had changed its mind, what there was of a mind of course.

Now why did the Monster change its mind?

I'll tell you why.

Because Hiccup was wearing his helmet.

It didn't want to start at the end with the long broken tickly thing on it.

Well, the Wodensfang and Toothless will be pleased about that, thought Hiccup, slightly hysterically. *They're always telling me not to forget the helmet...*

There was a click, click clicking noise.

Hiccup could not resist opening his left eyelid the smidgiest of a smidgeon.

He had seen many a strange and terrifying sight in his life, but this was one of the strangest and most terrifying.

Squinting down his own body, lubricated in a strange luminous material like a liquid shroud, he could see his own feet, and beyond them the Monster's head, opening its mouth and dislocating its jaws so it could take in Hiccup whole.

It began to swallow.

It is difficult to describe the sensation of being swallowed by a dragon. There really is nothing quite like it.

Apart from anything else, it makes the most disgusting *sound*, like a very rude liquidy slurping noise, and the feel of the suction pulling on your skin, as the mouth closes round your feet, and makes its way up your calves is both revoltingly wet, and also slightly painful.

It was really very difficult for Hiccup to stop himself from trembling, and keep his arms rammed to his sides.

UP the mouth moved, and Hiccup's feet began to burn like he was on fire, as the dragon's digestive juices began to work on him. Very, very slowly, the creature's mouth moved around his calves, inching its mouth over his limbs painfully, bit by bit.

Oh, Hiccup couldn't wait much longer, but he knew he would have to; the dragon had to reach his knees at least.

He sneaked a peek downwards. The animal had its arms stretched wide to steady itself, so its eyes couldn't see him if he suddenly sat up, but he had to wait until j-u-u-u-s-t the right moment...

It was agony by the time the mouth reached his knees.

Hiccup had the horrible feeling that his toes might be dissolving. He had lost the feeling in his right foot. But he had to strike at exactly the right moment...

As the disgusting monster's mouth crept over Hiccup's knees, Hiccup slow-ly, care-fully wriggled his left hand around the handle of Camicazi's spare sword.

The monster tensed, perhaps sensing the

infinitesimally small movement of his prey...

It lifted up its arms. All ten eyes were focused on Hiccup. Was it Hiccup's imagination, or did they see something there? Did they see something that made the Monster start, and the eyes open wide with amazement? And then as their talons poised to strike, the eyes on the talons opened wide with fury, and turned green and then black, as they suffused with blood...

Hiccup only had *one* second, *one* chance.

He sat up in one quick cat-like movement, reached out, and plunged his sword right in the middle of the creature's forehead.

For one awful moment Hiccup thought he might not have hit the right spot. Both the creature's arms sprang up and out. Hiccup hauled desperately on the sword to try and get it out again so he could strike once more but...

SQUERCH!!!

There was a small popping noise as the weak spot burst and...

WHHHOOOOOOOSHHHHHHHHHH!!!!!!!!

Out of the mouth Hiccup shot, because as the Monster died it let out a great shooting burst of sand and seawater and Hiccup raced on his back across the

slippery glass floor, landing upside down at the end of
the cavern in a swooshing tide of brine.

Even upside down, Hiccup could see that the
creature was dead, although it was still quivering and
jerking all over, but Hiccup didn't even stop to check,
he was so desperate to get the creature's digestive
juices off him. He rolled and rolled in the seawater,
rubbing and rubbing at his feet in particular, which
were still burning like they were on fire…

Eventually the burning died down until it became
almost bearable. The creature was lying quite still now.
Hiccup's poor feet were in a very bad state though,
he could see even in the dim Glow-worm light, and
the little toe on his left foot would never be the same
again. It had shrivelled into nothingness like a scraggly
little pink worm with the stuffing taken out of it, and
he couldn't move or feel it.

But at least it wasn't Hiccup's *head* that was a
scraggly little pink worm. *That* would have been a
disaster.

However, as he looked round the underground
cavern, Hiccup realised he was still in a serious fix.

He was in a glass cavern, underneath the sand,
and presumably up there on the surface the tide had
come in and so he was underneath the sea as well.

How was he going to get out of here?

But even as he was looking around at the extraordinary glass cavern, and the tunnels that ran off it, he had a tingling at the back of his head as a thought fell into place.

He reached into his fire-suit, and took out the raggedy remains of the map. It was looking a little worse for wear, that map, because like Hiccup himself, it had had rather a hard time of it. It was burnt, torn by poisoned fingernails, and covered in seawater and dragon digestive juices.

MAZE OF MIRRORS.

Oh for Thor's sake.

The red herring at the top of Grimbeard's map now seemed to be winking as well as laughing at him.

The Jewel was *here*.

Of course it was.

the wink of a red herring

24. THE WINK OF A RED HERRING

You know how it is.

You search high and low in the Archipelago for something, and it's only when you're looking for something *else* that you accidentally find it.

Squinting very hard at the map, Hiccup thought the lines and scribbles might indicate a way through the maze. Limping and slithering on the wet glass, Hiccup went through the exit of the cavern, and made his way through a warren of tunnels, following until the lair of the Monster opened out into a great glass chamber, and Hiccup let out a cry of wonder.

There it was, the Maze of Mirrors, the creature's secret chamber of treasures. How could such a primitive creature create something so very, very beautiful? Maybe the Wodensfang was right. There must be poetry, even in Monsters. For the glass in that chamber was woven with such artistry, and polished so fine that it had turned into mirrors. The ceiling was woven with glass like a spider's web, and then in the centre of the chamber was column after column of mirrored glass, as beautiful as columns on a Roman temple.

When you got closer still you could see, encased in the glass, the Monster's treasures that must have been stolen from generation after generation of poor Viking amber-collectors.

The Monster must have attacked Romans too, for there were gorgeous Roman silver cups floating in the columns like flies in amber. And speaking of amber, there was quantities and quantities of the stuff studded in the glass columns, the colour of honey, the colour of gold, the colour of fire, some with little creatures stuck in the golden liquid.

But Hiccup ran through that maze without even stopping, guided all the way by the squiggles on Grimbeard's map and his own gut. It was very confusing, just as confusing as looking into the eyes of a Triple-Header Deadly Shadow, for some of the columns were glass and some were mirror, and it was very difficult to tell what was see-through and what was a reflection.

On he slipped and slid through that sliding

mirror maze, searching, searching, for he knew what he was looking for now. And heart lifting with hope…

… he found it.

Wonder of wonders.

Water into stone.

A single glass column, shining, pure as a drop of water.

And right in the centre, suspended there as if it were floating, a little higher than Hiccup's eye level, was the dark red heart, the dark red Jewel… the Dragon's Jewel.

The Jewel that spelt the destruction of the dragons, and the humans' only hope.

The Jewel was hanging on a necklace, encased in the glass in such a way that it was as if the necklace was hanging on the neck of an invisible ghost. And as Hiccup circled round the column, nose pressed to the glass, his imagination filled in the torso of a gigantic bearded man: Grimbeard the Ghastly.

As Hiccup circled the column, he could just make out, on the golden backing of the necklace, the scratched initials: G.G.

Hiccup felt in his waistband for Camicazi's sword.

He took it out and took a good aim at the

column of glass about a foot or so below where the Jewel was suspended, swinging at it with all his might, as if he were swinging at a tree in the Hooligan forest.

The first swing took a big glass chunk out of the column.

The second, a larger bite.

And on the third swing of the sword Hiccup ducked as the entire column of glass came down with an almighty musical crash, tinkling little pieces raining down on him, and the echoes ringing out in that gigantic underground mirrored cavern like a pealing of bells.

Before Hiccup reached out to take it, he hesitated.

What if he were to take the Jewel, and it were then to fall into the wrong hands?

But what if he did not take the Jewel, and there was nothing then to stop the anger of the Dragon Furious?

He put his head in his hands.

How I wish that I were not the one who finds the Lost Things! thought Hiccup passionately. *Why does it have to be me who makes these choices?*

Most of us are lucky not to be Kings and Heroes, because we do not have to make the choices that

Kings and Heroes have to make.

Hiccup chose to take the Jewel.

Hiccup tore a piece off his shirt and wrapped his hand in it so he could draw the Jewel out of the mound of shards of glass.

He held it up, so that the light shone brilliantly off the golden amber depths, and carefully swept off the powdered glass with one finger before putting the amber Jewel around his neck and dropping it down his fire-suit so it wasn't visible.

And then he said:

'Thank you, Grimbeard the Ghastly.'

I don't know why he said it, for there was no one there of course.

But there was a beat of about two seconds.

And the hairs on the back of Hiccup's head stood up.

'Hic-cup...' said a faint, spooky, echoing voice. 'Hic-cup...'

Oh for Thor's sake.

What was that?

It couldn't be the voice of the Dragon Furious, could it? Hiccup's mind went back to the Dragon chasing him through the cave warren of the Flashburn School of Swordfighting.

No, it couldn't be…

But so spooky, so echoey was the voice that for one mad minute Hiccup thought it might be the ghost of Grimbeard the Ghastly, come back to haunt him for taking his Jewel.

'Hic-cup… Hic-cup… Answer me… Hic-cup…'

And then, Hiccup stopped dead and started to run back through the cavern, checking column after column.

'Hic-cup… Hic-cup…'

The voice was weak, despairing.

There, in one cloudy glass column was the outline of a human boy.

A boy like himself.

Was it just a trick of the echoing mirror maze?

Hiccup pressed his palm against the glass.

And as if the boy were a mirror image of himself, a hand on the other side of the glass pressed back, hand-to-hand.

Gently Hiccup pushed his forehead with the Slavemark on it on the glass. And as the boy

302

inside the column dropped
his head forward too, the
two Slavemarks touched, on
either side the glass.

The boy was Fishlegs.

25. I DON'T THINK I'M DEAD...

Fishlegs's weary face was looking back at him through the smoky glass of the column.

'Oh, Fishlegs!' cried Hiccup. 'I thought that you were dead!'

'No,' said Fishlegs. 'I'm not dead. At least... I don't *think* I'm dead...'

His voice was very, very weak.

'Though I have to admit, I'm not feeling at my most lively. What with one thing and another I've had better weeks in the Archipelago.'

Hiccup laughed, shakily. 'No, you're not dead, Fishlegs. You're in the lair of the Monster of the Amber Slavelands. The Monster likes eating fresh meat so it must have been keeping you alive.'

'Ah,' said Fishlegs. 'I knew I had a feeling I wasn't in a great situation...'

'Lean against the other side of the column, Fishlegs,' Hiccup ordered, and he began to swing his axe, gingerly cutting through one side of the glass column, being very, very careful, for he did not want to hurt Fishlegs when it broke.

Thor's birthday, it was cold down there. Hiccup shivered as he swung his axe, the damp seeping through his sandals, the cold of the underground glass tunnels penetrating right into his heart.

'Put your hands over your head, Fishlegs,' whispered Hiccup. (He didn't know why he was whispering – the Monster was dead but it was SPOOKY down there, in the dark, in the cold.)

Chunk! Chunk! Two more swings of the axe and the glass column encasing Fishlegs fell away. His friend was standing there, curled over in a slight ball, his hands over his head. Slowly he brought down his arms.

It was as if Hiccup was bringing a frozen statue into life. A bedraggled, weary figure he was. Tear-stained, rags flapping around him like the tatters of a scarecrow ripped to shreds, nearly blue with cold, his smashed glasses falling off his nose.

A bedraggled weary figure he was.

Hiccup was the very mirror-image of him.

Neither of them were Vikings now. Lost Tribes, lost dragons, lost everything. Hungry, thin as brooms, the Slavemarks proclaiming their slavedom, both runts, the two boys stood looking at each other, swaying on their feet.

Fishlegs was cold as ice, and Hiccup rubbed his purple arms, trying to get his circulation going.

'What are you doing here?' asked Fishlegs through chattering teeth.

'Looking for you…'

'But I'm not important,' said Fishlegs weakly and drearily. 'You ought to be on your Quest… Your destiny. What about the Dragon Jewel?'

'You *are* important!' said Hiccup, urgently trying to bring him back to life, by rubbing his arms, his chest, *anything* to try and warm him up. 'Your lobster-claw necklace saved my life.'

'Really?' said Fishlegs. He opened his eyes in disbelief. '*My* necklace saved YOUR life?'

So Hiccup told Fishlegs the

My necklace saved your life?

306

story of his mother, Termagant, and the Stealth Dragon, and the lobster pot lost in the mist fourteen years before.

Who says stories cannot bring things to life?

That story brought Fishlegs to life, all right.

He turned from grey to a pale pink, and his heartbeat, so faint, flickered back into a steady rhythm.

'So my mother, she *did* love me after all!' said Fishlegs, in surprise. 'She wanted the best for me. She wanted to meet me again, on Hero's End!'

'And she would have done,' said Hiccup, 'if she had lived. And the Deadly Shadow dragon who has sworn to look after you, is now *your* Deadly Shadow.'

Fishlegs had spent his whole life having the worst of everything.

He had the embarrassingly vegetarian hunting-dragon, the riding-dragon that was the size of a Shetland pony. He had been bottom of the class in absolutely everything, plus he had eczema, asthma, knock-knees and short-sight. So it was a pretty amazing moment to discover that somewhere out there is a triple-headed, armed-to-the-teeth, ridiculously cool Deadly Shadow dragon that had sworn to look after you, and lay down its life for you.

For the final boost, Hiccup drew out of his

waistcoat... the Dragon Jewel.

It shone like a warm golden star in the darkness of that glass cavern.

'Oh...' breathed Fishlegs. He put out a hand and touched it. 'The Dragon Jewel,' whispered Fishlegs. He looked up at Hiccup...

... and smiled, with excitement, for the first time in a long time.

'Hiccup, this really has got to mean that you are the King.'

Hiccup smiled back awkwardly. 'Well, it means I'm pretty good at finding the King's Lost Things, anyway. But don't forget, you were here first.'

Fishlegs stroked the Dragon Jewel for a few moments.

And then slowly, he got to his feet.

'Right,' said Fishlegs.

He pushed his smashed glasses determinedly and securely on to his nose. 'Now we have to get out of here. I just can't miss everybody seeing me on the back of a Triple-Header Deadly Shadow dragon, I'm sorry, it's just too good a moment.'

We have to get out of here.

Hiccup grinned, and took out the blasted, ragged, burnt and soaked remains of the disintegrated map to look for the way out.

The two boys walked through the tunnels until they found the one that Grimbeard had helpfully marked as the exit.

And as they walked, the tunnels seemed to be leading higher and higher, and there was a strange light that wasn't the light of Electricsquirms or Electricstickys or Glow-worms, which had lit the cavern below, and suddenly the light felt as if it were all around them. And on the other side of the glass there were suddenly fern-shapes, moving and waving...

Seaweed.

The glass tunnel had emerged out of the sand and they were under the sea at the bottom of the ocean. Great drifts and shoals of fish drifted past, swimming in and out of the seaweed. Gentle jellyfish softly floated by, and as the tunnel moved up it left the seabed like a great glass snake, and they could see crabs scuttling below them.

'Wow.' Fishlegs pressed his nose up to the glass.

The tunnel went up sharply now, and they slid so much they couldn't get a grip. Hiccup had to carve little nicks into the glass so they could get a foothold.

They were just in time, as it happens, for the tunnel had one little loop that the sea had not yet covered. Once the tide covered it and the tunnel was entirely underwater, they would not have been able to break the tunnel without the ocean rushing in and drowning them.

But there it was, one lovely little loop that was surrounded only by pure air.

Hiccup broke the tunnel with his axe, and carefully they climbed over the broken shards and into the surrounding ocean.

It was cold, that sea.

As they looked around them, they were just two little heads bobbing beside the broken tunnel in the middle of a vast expanse of ocean. Sea, sea, sea, as far as the eye could see...

The tide had come in completely.

They had walked even further than Hiccup thought – a mile, maybe more – into the open ocean. To the west Hiccup could see a little smudgy grey outline that must be land, the land of the island of Swallow.

'I'm never going to make it...' gasped Fishlegs. He was already turning blue again.

'You will make it,' said Hiccup between

chattering teeth. 'Swim!'

And he began to swim himself, towards that
smudgy grey outline on the very distant horizon.
'Swim! Swim! Swim! You *must* make it...'

But the vast echoing sea was so large, and they
were so small, and the distant land mass was so very,
very far away...

SWIM! Fishlegs,
SWIM!

26. A GHOST FROM THE PAST

Sometimes our little human splashings are not enough.

However hard we try, however strong our heroic human wills (and us humans have such a capacity, such a heroic capacity for believing that the impossible might be possible), sometimes our ridiculously puny human arms are too weak. Sometimes the world is just too big for us, the hurricane too wild, the sea so huge, that it wears out even the bravest of hearts, the strongest of wills.

So it would have been with Fishlegs and Hiccup, I have to tell you – they would have drowned that day in the seas around the Amber Slavelands, despite everything, despite their miraculous escape from the Maze of Mirrors and the lair of the Slitherfang. Hiccup would have sunk to the ocean floor with the Dragon Jewel around his neck, and this story would have had a very different kind of ending.

If it hadn't been for one thing.

That one thing was flying right now on invisible wings, above the oceans of the Amber Slavelands, searching, searching.

A ghost from the past.

A ghost that was hoping to make amends, a ghost

that was never going to give up because of the promise
he made to Fishlegs's mother.

The Deadly Shadow would not give up.

'There is always hope,' whispered Innocence.
'Remember the last time this happened we gave up,
and Fisshlegss was still alive? You have to learn from
stories. We will not give up this time...'

Even the boundless optimism of Camicazi, riding
on the back of the Deadly Shadow, was fading.

Of course it was, for had she not seen with her
very own eyes, Hiccup dragged down under the sands
by some terrifying eyes-on-claws monster?

With a howl of terror, the Deadly Shadow had
dug at the spot with his great claws, and she had dived
down and joined in with her own pathetic human
hands, digging, digging, digging at the spot they last
saw him.

But sometimes the world is too big even for
dragon claws. The Deadly Shadow was an Air Dragon,
not a Sea Dragon, not an Earth Dweller – he was
not built for burrowing. He could not follow Hiccup
underneath the sand, however hard he dug. But on, on,
he and Camicazi dug, until the great tide swept in, and
swallowed up their pathetic diggings, their pointless
hole and turned the world to water.

Hours and hours they searched the world-now-turned-to-ocean.

I do not know what moral you can take from this apart from one: they carried on, even though all hope was lost, for it was impossible that Hiccup should have survived being buried deep under sand and under ocean.

'But perhaps he wriggled out of the Monster's claws at the last moment,' said Camicazi to the Deadly Shadow. 'Trust me, guys, I have seen Hiccup survive so many other impossible situations...'

But yet again, this seemed like even more of an impossible situation to survive than the last one.

Nonetheless, they carried on, and it was good that they did, for as we know, despite all odds, Hiccup *had* survived, and he and Fishlegs needed them now.

The Deadly Shadow had gone back in time.

He had forgotten that thirteen years had passed.

It was as if it were that very same day that he promised his human, Termagant: 'By our bright-green blood and our shining claws, we will keep your baby safe.'

Just such a day it had been, a day of blue, with just a hint of clouds on the edge of the world.

'We promise... We promise...' Patience muttered

to the others in Dragonese. 'We promise, Termagant, we will keep your baby safe...'

'We promisse... We promissse...' Arrogance and Innocence whispered back.

Swooping over the blue expanse of ocean, the endless waves that stretched for ever, they searched for a little lobster pot, bobbing on the waves. Their six Deadly Shadow eyes, the sharpest eyes in the world, the eyes that can see a nanodragon moving from a distance of half a mile, clicking, clicking, scanning the ocean. Their senses all alert.

Then, with panic rising, they could feel the clouds moving in, suddenly, a mist beginning to form... Surely history could not be about to repeat itself? Surely this was a day of second chances?

They swooped down further, desperately looking for the little lobster pot. And the Deadly Shadow found it.

Way down below, a flicker of movement, a smudge of pink, of human life, a tiny wriggle on the endless stretch of blue.

Down the Deadly Shadow swooped, joy leaping in his camouflaged breast, and as they soared closer, Camicazi could see it too, and she let out a joyful whoop.

A smashed and broken lobster pot, attached to the back of a boy swimming, a boy with a lobster-claw necklace around his neck. The boy was supporting another boy with broken glasses, and even at the height it was flying, the dragon could see in the face of that boy, the smudged and vague outline, the wet bedraggled memory of a human it had loved.

Termagant's child!

'We'll meet again, Termagant! We'll
meet again!' snorted the three heads of the Deadly
Shadow triumphantly, shooting out bolts of lightning
as he swooped ever downwards.

'We're being attacked!' whispered Fishlegs, shielding his eyes and looking upwards, as the Deadly Shadow made a rather clumsy crash-landing beside them, due to over-excitement.

Hiccup and Fishlegs were nearly dead, and the shock of a highly camouflaged dragon landing nearly right on top of them out of the blue, practically finished them off. But as they gasped and coughed up water, the dragon plucked them out of the sea and deposited them on his back, still gasping and coughing up water... but alive.

'I don't believe it!' crowed Camicazi, with shining eyes. 'I mean, I *do* believe it, because you've done it so many times before, but this time I really... do... not... believe... it...'

Hiccup smiled because he didn't really believe it himself either, what with one thing and another, and panting, he drew the Dragon Jewel out of his waistcoat.

Well of course, Camicazi couldn't believe *that* even more than anything else. She made him take it out, and put it back again, and he let her hold it, and she turned it over and over, saying: 'I DO NOT BELIEVE IT... I DO NOT BELIEVE IT... How do you do it?

'What are you going to do with it?' asked Camicazi.

Hiccup sighed. 'I'm not quite sure,' he admitted. 'I have to think of some way to use it so that I can stop this war.

'Fishlegs,' said Hiccup, as the dragon took off into the sky, 'this is your mother's dragon, the Deadly Shadow. The head on the left is Innocence, the head on the right is Arrogance, and the one in the middle is Patience, because that's what he has to have.'

Fishlegs was sprawled on the Deadly Shadow's back, holding on for dear life, his clothes already steaming as the dragon's back was as warm as an oven. He felt his whole body coming back to life.

'How do you do?' whispered Fishlegs. 'Excuse me if I don't sit up... I'm a bit tired.'

Something about this dragon made him feel secure, and even in his weakened state he struggled to sit up, the wind blowing back his wet hair, the Slavemark burning bright on his forehead. 'So... *you* are my mother's dragon?'

'I was!' sang the Deadly Shadow. 'But now I am yours. Yours for ever. I promise I will never leave you. I am at your service... I will serve you faithfully, from now until death.'

Hiccup translated.

Wow…

Fishlegs's back straightened. His eyes shone. Things were looking up. He, Fishlegs, the ex-most-despised-member-of-the-Hooligan-Tribe, the slave, the orphan and runt, was now the proud owner of literally the coolest dragon he had ever seen. 'And my mother… was a Chief's daughter?' asked Fishlegs.

'The best and truest human that I ever met,' said Patience.

'She was a poet, too,' explained Hiccup. 'And half-Berserk, as we always thought.'

Even in his ragged, hungry, cold state, this put so much heart into Fishlegs. His mother was a poet! That must be where he got his bard-skills from. His father was a Hero! Well, that was a bit of a mystery, but…

… *finally* he knew who he was.

FINALLY

Fishlegs
knew who
he was.

Long - Eared Caretaker Dragon

~ STATISTICS ~

FEAR FACTOR: 3
ATTACK: 6
SPEED: 4
SIZE: 5
DISOBEDIENCE: 1

These dragons
make excellent
guard-dogs and
babysitters. Fishlegs
was looked after by
one of these dragons
when he was a baby.

Relax for a Second...

If you want to end the story here, please feel free.
In a way it would be best.
For what could be a happier ending than this, the three
friends soaring up into the clouds, the Dragon Jewel
safe around Hiccup's neck?
It has been a long, long day, and that really should
be the end of it.
But I have to confess...
... it isn't.
So if you really *do* want to carry on to the bitter end,
I suggest, dear reader, that you take a little break
for a moment.
Drink a large glass of water. Have a nibble of
something sustaining, with slow release energy,
a snack perhaps with oats in it.
Relax for a second.
There.
Then here we go...

27. THE STORY ENDS AS IT BEGAN...

This story, you see, began with Hiccup being ambushed by his mother, Valhallarama.

And that is also how it ends.

Nobody can track a Deadly Shadow dragon.

Nobody except for... Valhallarama.

Nobody can see one, so beautifully camouflaged are they... But Valhallarama, that indomitable breath-holding action woman, flew so high, to such airy pinnacles of thinning cloud, that she was looking *down* at them, not up, and she saw, not the Deadly Shadow, but the three little humans clinging to the back of nothing.

The three friends did not see her coming.

The Deadly Shadow's senses were dulled slightly, perhaps by the exhilaration of the moment, and the fact that it was not expecting danger. Deadly Shadows do not expect to be attacked, because something so scary very rarely is.

Perhaps Arrogance caught a shining silver streak of movement, screaming just above his eye-level that caused him to stiffen and look up.

But it was too late.

Valhallarama and the Silver Phantom, hiding high in a cloud-bank, swooped down in a rocketing silver howl, like a bright avenging Fury, the unstoppable, relentless, screaming hand of Fate. Valhallarama's metal arm reached out and she plucked her son from the back of the camouflaged Deadly Shadow with the casual ease that she had plucked him, two weeks before, from the back of the Windwalker.

The Silver Phantom rocketed on towards Darkheart, unstoppable, uncatchable, for in open skies the Silver Phantom was the fastest riding-dragon in the entire world.

Guiding the Phantom with her knees alone, she held Hiccup with one hand, and with the other she took the Dragon Jewel on its necklace from around Hiccup's neck, and placed it around her own.

Hiccup, swinging from his mother's stern unyielding arm, was as shocked as if he had been dunked suddenly in a tub of ice-cold water.

And once he had got over *that*, he was angry.

Oh, by Loki's little lunatic leg-warmers, he was angry.

'*What are you* DOING?' Hiccup roared up at that unforgiving metal mask looming over him, looking sternly, unwaveringly down at her target of Darkheart.

'I am not a child any more, how dare you treat me like this?

'I mean I don't expect you to be HELPFUL or anything, why would I expect that? You've never BEEN THERE! Years and years of leaving my father and me on our own, YEARS AND YEARS AND YEARS! Not always answering my letters... Going away even when I beg you not to... Not listening when I speak...'

Purple in the face, kicking out with his legs, Hiccup yelled, 'I've got used to that over the years!

I've *had* to get used to it! But the one thing I *don't* expect,' bellowed Hiccup, 'the one thing I don't expect, is for you to actually BETRAY me... Is that really too much to ask?'

And there was a great deal more where that came from, for when fourteen years of frustrated fury comes out, it tends to come out in a rush.

But Valhallarama did not answer. She carried on, regardless, grim, unyielding. They blasted through the sky in a blinding silver rush of Hiccup's boiling anger and Valhallarama's righteous determination.

Nothing was going to stop her.

She was taking Hiccup back, back, back to face the music in the Prison of Darkheart.

28. FACING THE MUSIC...
AND ALVIN AND THE WITCH

Night had fallen in the Amber Slavelands.

Outside the prison walls, the air was screaming with dragons. The sentries along the walls were barely holding them back.

The courtyard of Prison Darkheart was brilliantly lit with flares. In the centre of the courtyard sat Alvin the Treacherous and his mother, seated on twin thrones.

Hundreds and hundreds of Warriors of the Wilderwest and slaves stood carrying flaming torches in their hands. The atmosphere was grim. Every soul in that prison was listening tensely to the dragon apocalypse outside.

Alvin had called this Grand Meeting of soldiers, slaves, warriors and everybody, in order to conduct a few executions to work off some of his anger at the loss of Hiccup earlier in the day.

But they were interrupted in this amiable diversion by an unexpected visitor. Over those battlements flew the Silver Phantom, and on the Phantom's back was Valhallarama the Hero, and swinging from just one of his mother's metal arms,

was the infuriated Hiccup.

'Don't shoot! Hold your fire!' cried Alvin the Treacherous, for he with his quick one eye had already spotted the Dragon Jewel burning bright around Valhallarama's neck.

King Alvin's face lit up with sudden joy. 'Mother!' he gasped. 'She's got the Jewel!'

The white witch stood up a little higher, her hair trailing behind her in a blaze of glory. 'I knew it!' she spat triumphantly. 'I knew all my calculations could not be wrong!'

The Silver Phantom circled round the courtyard once, twice, glowing bright as the moon.

And then he landed on his back legs, placing Hiccup carefully on the ground before the witch, and Valhallarama leapt lightly from the Phantom's back and stood there beside him.

Hiccup threw himself away from her, shook her arm off him as if it were poisonous, still too angry with her to be frightened.

The Phantom was limping slightly from an arrow wound in his foreleg.

The crowd was silent until they spotted the Dragon Jewel around Valhallarama's neck.

'The Jewel! She has the Jewel! We're saved!'

All around the courtyard the crowd began to cheer: 'VAL-HALL-ARA-MA! VAL-HALL-ARA-MA! She has the Jewel!'

Valhallarama was the most popular Hero in the Archipelago, even more famous than Humungously Hotshot or Flashburn. And she had found them the Jewel! Even the slaves were rattling their chains in appreciation.

Valhallarama reached for her iron helmet and took it off, throwing it into the crowd, so that all could see her face.

A proud white face, cut as if it were made of granite. Daunting to look upon, like a particularly stern cliff.

And then she stood with her arms crossed in silence.

'Leave it to me, Alvin,' hissed the witch, trying to see through that suit of armour, that granite face, to what might be Valhallarama's weaknesses. 'Leave it to Mother... This is a slightly sensitive situation, and it calls for a witch's tongue...'

It *was* a slightly sensitive situation – a mother delivering not only the Jewel but her son to his likely death.

THREE cheers FOR VaLHallarama!

'Congratulations, Valhallarama!' said the witch, holding up one bony white arm in salutation.

'I have to confess, Valhallarama,' continued the witch, 'I underestimated you. I did not tell you that the Traitor of the Wilderwest was your own son, in case you let family feeling get in the way of your duty. I should have known that a great Hero like yourself would put your Kingdom above mere personal whims. Three cheers for Valhallarama!'

The courtyard rocked with applause.

Valhallarama said nothing.

'Give Alvin the Jewel that will save us all, Valhallarama,' said the witch, trying to sound casual and as if it were not an order.

But Valhallarama did not give Alvin the Jewel.

Instead, she withdrew a single arrow from her quiver. An arrow with black raven feathers on it. She twirled it round and round on one finger, thoughtfully.

Valhallarama said nothing, her Hero's face impassive as she twirled that arrow round and round.

There is a power in silence, especially when you have as charismatic a presence as Valhallarama.

The power of silence is that it forces others to speak.

The witch moistened her lips, her half-blind eyes taking in the movement of the arrow.

'I see you have the arrow that an unknown soldier may have accidentally shot your Silver Phantom with, after the Phantom so very kindly delivered us the map...' said the witch smoothly. 'We are so glad that it did not hurt him badly, aren't we, Alvin?'

Alvin showed his teeth in a charming smile. 'My relief is beyond words.'

'It was an accident. We were furious with the soldier in question. Indeed, he lost his life. I need not tell you, Valhallarama, that our promise that we gave you still holds,' purred the witch. 'Alvin promises that if you give him the Dragon Jewel, he will use it merely as a *threat*, not to destroy the dragons for ever. Is that not so, Alvin?'

'Word of a Treacherous,' smiled Alvin.

'Unless of course,' the witch continued, sweet and smooth as butter, 'the Dragon Furious gives us no choice...' She shrugged her shoulders, indicating the roar of the Rebellion outside. 'Alvin is realistic, and he would have the strength to act decisively if he is forced. Look around you at the Archipelago. Our perfect world, burnt to a crisp by dragon fire. The dragons would kill us all!'

Hiccup could keep quiet no longer. He turned on the witch.

'It is YOU who have inflamed that situation!' yelled Hiccup passionately. 'I have seen your dragon-traps! Destroying dragon eggs, killing them in their thousands with your explosive weapons! No wonder so many dragons have joined the Rebellion!'

Hiccup's words rang out in the courtyard.

'And I ask you, what is this perfect world that you are talking about? Is it perfect to have humans and dragons dying in chains?'

Is it perfect to have humans and dragons dying in CHAINS?

Hiccup pointed at the Silver Phantom.

'Are creatures as beautiful as this to be made extinct for all time?' cried Hiccup.

'Are dragons never to sail through the skies again, on jewel-coloured airy wings, or light up the world once more with the glory of their fiery breath?

'Are we to say goodbye for ever to the magic, and the dreaming and the flying of our childhoods?

'I say NO!' cried Hiccup, red in the face, shaking his fist.

'Dragons should be free, just as every single human being in this building should be free!'

I say NO! Dragons and humans should be FREE!

All around, the crowd was murmuring to each other like an unhappy sea.

Valhallarama twirled that black arrow in her hand, faster and faster, listening intently, with her head on one side.

'So speaks your son, Valhallarama, Hiccup the *slave!*' sneered the witch, even whiter than ever.

'Like father, like son, for I know you will be

shocked when I tell you, Valhallarama, your husband, Stoick the Vast, has also become a slave.'

The witch pointed out poor Stoick, who was looking at the ground.

But still Valhallarama said nothing.

Why won't she speak? thought the witch, feeling increasingly desperate.

She sent out her words like poisoned arrows, still trying to find that fatal weakness in Valhallarama's armour.

'I feel saddened for you, Valhallarama, such a Great Hero as you are,' sorrowed the witch pityingly, 'that your family has let you down so badly, and brought disgrace upon their Tribe and the Kingdom.'

And now the witch looked very crafty.

'But then, I read your destiny when you were a little girl, and you were never meant to marry Stoick, were you, Valhallarama? Stoick the Vast was never worthy of *you*...' cooed the witch in her sweetest voice.

Valhallarama's face did not change. You could not tell for one second what she was thinking. Round and round the arrow whirled, faster and faster, as if it were a spinner in a game, and no one knew where it would stop in the end.

'If circumstances had not intervened with destiny, you would have married Humungously Hotshot the Hero, a man of your own calibre, and if you had done so, none of this would have happened: the second-best husband, the unfortunate runt son, the disaster that has hit the Archipelago,' sighed the witch.

'It's tragic, really. I cannot bear to think of your girlish disappointment, waiting and waiting for a Hero who never came.' The witch shook her head sorrowfully. 'A maiden's tears are so particularly touching. It positively melts my witch's heart to think of it.'

Excellinor paused. 'But then, time moves on, does it not? I hear Humungous has married at last, a lady twenty years your junior.'

Valhallarama did not react.

The witch gave a cruel smile. 'What a shame destiny has taken such a crooked course. But now you have a chance to move on yourself and put things right, Valhallarama. Look, see how Fate has marked my son Alvin out as our saviour, by giving him eight of the Things already!'

The witch finished her speech with a final ringing flourish. 'You are a woman of sense and principle. You brought us the map because you knew that this was right, and you could help us stop this war that has torn our perfect world apart. We want to put that world back together again, make it good as new. And who knows? Perhaps without certain things it might be even more perfect. Complete your Quest, Valhallarama. Fulfil your destiny and give Alvin the Jewel!'

For Thor's sake, surely the great metal she-mountain has to speak NOW? *thought the witch. Has she gone dumb? The suspense is killing me.*

Valhallarama put up her mighty hand. At last, she stepped forward. She spoke.

And herein again, lies the power of silence. When a person who has been quiet speaks, people tend to listen.

The crowd leant forward to make sure they caught every single word of what she was saying.

'The witch has said her piece, and now I shall say mine,' said Valhallarama.

'I have been absent from the Archipelago's history for some considerable time. What I am about to offer you is an explanation for my absence, and I am not explaining this to you, witch, or you, Alvin, or even to you, the assembled Tribes of the Archipelago.'

She bowed to the silent watching crowds, and those crowds include us, the readers, the listeners, the invisible watchers of this story.

'I am explaining this to my son Hiccup,' said Valhallarama.

She turned to her son Hiccup, who was still standing with his fists clenched, bursting with anger, and she looked straight at him.

'I have spent most of my life Questing,' said Valhallarama.

'When I was a child my father, the soothsayer Old Wrinkly, foretold to me in secret that the Archipelago would face a dreadful peril and the only one who could avert it would be a new King of the Wilderwest. He told me the Prophecy of the King's Lost Things, kept a secret only among the wise, so that the Things should not be found by one who is unworthy.

'I was brave, I was intelligent, I knew that I was

worthy. My father had brought me up as a Hero, and a potential King, and though my father's dreams went awry as many parents' dreams do, secretly, I dedicated the rest of my life to Questing for those Things.

'And perhaps,' sighed Valhallarama, 'if I am entirely honest, and since this is a moment for telling the truth, it was also because there is a wandering spirit in me, and I was too much a Viking, to stay too much at home.

'My husband Stoick understood the importance of my Quest to me even though I never told him why I was Questing or what I was Questing for.

'I would call that *real* True Love,' said Valhallarama, 'which is beyond the comprehension of both maidens and of witches.

'Nonetheless, I cannot begin to tell you how much I have sacrificed in the pursuit of my Quest,' said Valhallarama. 'Do not think that just because I have the soul of a soldier, and cannot speak soft words, that it was not hard for me, or that because I left, I did not love.

'Year after year away from home, away from my loved ones, my husband, my son. The monsters I have fought, the Warriors I have battled, flying so far to the north, south, west, and east, it felt like I must have crossed the whole world, sleeping in trees, in caves, in ice-houses, wandering for so long on my own I nearly forgot my own language.'

Slowly, Hiccup's fists unclenched, just a tiny, tiny bit, for this was reminding him of the loneliness of his own Quest over the last year.

'But when the Quest is for the future of the Archipelago itself,' said Valhallarama, 'terrible sacrifices sometimes have to be made.

'And in this case the sacrifice was bitter indeed, for however hard I searched, whatever lead I followed, I did not find one single Thing. Not one.

'So when the witch told me that her son Alvin had *eight* of the King's Lost Things, why this news took my breath away.

'I was stunned. What a very great Hero this Alvin must be to have succeeded where all my strength and intelligence had failed! Reluctantly I stood back for the King that fortune foretold, and agreed to acquire the map for the King so that he could search for the Dragon Jewel.'

'Yes, well, you were quite right,' said the witch hurriedly. 'My Alvin is something special.'

'But what you forgot to tell me, witch, and I am sure it was an unintentional oversight,' drawled

Valhallarama sarcastically, 'was that it was *my son*
HICCUP who found the Things first. I was so busy
peering for the Things at the farthest corners of the
earth, that I did not notice what was happening right
under my nose at home. While I was searching for
those Things with the utmost of my power and strength
and brilliance, the Things were making their way to
Hiccup, quietly, effortlessly, and without him even
realising.'

'Hiccup may find the Things,' hissed the witch,
'but it is *my son* ALVIN who ends up with them in the
end, notice!'

Valhallarama ignored the witch. 'I began to
ask myself some questions when I had got over the
headache caused by my son very understandably
dropping a tree trunk on my head.'

'Did Hiccup drop a tree trunk on your head?'
interrupted Alvin, cheering up for a second. 'Can I just
say that that is typical? Absolutely typical.'

'The tree trunk rearranged my thoughts,' said
Valhallarama, 'along with the surprise caused by my
Phantom returning with a black arrow in his foreleg.

'I found myself thinking:

'Why did the Things find their way to Hiccup
rather than to me? Was it because in my endless Quest

to save the Archipelago, I had forgotten to ask the questions that make a King a King?

'And is it, in fact, the Questions that are more important than the Quest?

'Perhaps,' (here again Valhallarama sighed) 'I had to face the cold facts, dropping on me like a tree trunk from above. Destiny had not chosen me for King because for all my intelligence, I did not have the sympathetic mind that could ask such questions in the first place...

'You see, the Hooligan Tribe has never had slaves. But we have stood by and let other Tribes take slaves. We have closed our eyes to the misery of places such as this, the great Prison Darkheart. We have pretended that they do not really exist.

'But my son Hiccup did not pretend that they did not exist. Is that what a King is?

'And then, you see, there is the Question of the dragons. My son put that rather neatly, don't you think, witch?' said Valhallarama proudly. 'Are we to say goodbye for ever, to the magic and the dreaming and the flying of our childhoods?'

'A childish Question, perhaps, that could only be put by a child. For it is too late, already,' hissed the witch, her smile a death-grin. 'The war has, regretfully, gone too far to save the dragons from extinction. It is, you see, a Question of Them or Us...'

'It may, indeed, be too late,' admitted Valhallarama grimly, her voice smooth and cold as steel, her eyes like bullets. 'But at least my son would *try* to save the glory of the dragons that I love.

'There are some dragons that are monsters,' admitted Valhallarama.

'But then there are also some *humans* who are monsters.' (And at this point she paused and looked significantly at Alvin the Treacherous and the witch.) 'On the back of the Silver Phantom I have flown so high that his wing-tips seemed to touch the very moon itself...

On the back of the Silver
Phantom I have flown so high
his wing-tips seemed to touch the
very moon itself...

'Are dragons like my Silver Phantom to be destroyed just because there are some dragons out there that are monsters? Are we to be for ever earthbound because the dragons are no more?'

Obligingly, the Silver Phantom slowly opened his bright wings to their utmost extent and the rising moon lit up all of his delicate silver scales so that they shone like stars.

The crowd caught their breath longingly, remembering flying through the stormy skies of the Archipelago on the back of their own dragons.

'And while I am on the subject of the Silver Phantom,' said Valhallarama, conversationally, stern eyes narrowing, fingers spinning, spinning, spinning the arrow, 'I thought I might bring up something which has been puzzling me.

'This arrow that I have taken from my Phantom's leg that the witch claims was from an unknown soldier, is flighted with raven feathers and dipped in the poison of the Venomous Vorpent.

'I believe you keep ravens as pets, witch, and the poison of the Vorpent is your poison of choice?'

Yes, I remember reading her destiny now, thought the witch with disagreeable surprise. *And even at seven years old she was a wild, but also repellently clever, little girl... That must be where the horrible little Hiccup brat gets his brains from, because it's certainly not from his idiotic father...*

'A raven does make a lovely pet,' admitted the witch. 'But I am trying not to use Vorpent poison as much actually – it isn't as effective as it used to be...'

'You lied, witch, didn't you?' persisted Valhallarama. 'This arrow belongs to your son Alvin, and it was he who shot my Phantom.'

Silence.

The witch's tongue had run out of lies.

Valhallarama turned back to the crowd.

'You do have a choice of Kings here, peoples of the Archipelago,' said Valhallarama. 'Don't let anybody tell you that you do not have a choice.

'You can choose the lying witch's son, Alvin, the man with the golden nose, the blood-soaked hook and the empty heart.'

She pointed at Alvin, a splendid muscly, Emperor-like figure, it has to be admitted, and so bedecked with the Lost Things, it was almost ridiculous.

'And you know in your heart of hearts what this man Alvin is offering you.

'Or you can choose my own son, Hiccup, who is not a runt, but something special, and who offers you the hope of a new and better world.'

Or you can choose my own
son, Hiccup, who is not a runt,
but something special.

She turned to Hiccup.

Hiccup's anger had now entirely gone, and he felt a great calmness, as if some great weight had left him.

'I love you, Hiccup, although my stiff lips will not let me make the kind words I hear other mothers speaking,' said Vallhallarama with difficulty.

'I cannot change or regret the wandering Warrior I am. But by Thor's thunder, I can fight for you, with all my Warrior heart, and this is one thing that I truly excel at.'

The black arrow was now whirring so fast in Valhallarama's fingers that it was just a blur.

'The witch has spoken on behalf of Alvin, and I have spoken on behalf of Hiccup. And now we all have to make our choice, peoples of the Archipelago,' said Valhallarama.

'And this is mine.'

Valhallarama's choice was pretty decisive.

So quick you could hardly see it, for a true Hero's fingers can move as fast as thought, Valhallarama loaded that spinning arrow with black feathers, and shot it straight at Alvin's heart.

She took the Dragon Jewel from around her own neck and placed it around the neck of her son, Hiccup Horrendous Haddock the Third.

Uproar in the courtyard.

The witch shrieked.

Alvin staggered, but the arrow did not penetrate the three chunky metal breast plates he wore under his royal garments. (Alvin was intelligent enough to realise he had made a few enemies in his time.)

'I'm fine, Mother,' he assured her, yanking out the arrow from the breastplates with some difficulty. He was purple with temper. 'But we need to stop talking now and kill everybody.'

'I'm dealing with this, Alvin,' spat the witch.

'It's a delicate situation.

'THE KING IS FINE!' screeched Excellinor. She was rattled right off her perch now. 'You'll be relieved to hear that THE KING IS FINE! NOBODY MOVE! NOBODY PANIC! WE ARE COMPLETELY IN CHARGE HERE!'

She put out her arms, like giant bat wings, trying to regain control of the situation.

Her voice dripped with acid.

'We will overlook your attempted murder of my son, Valhallarama,' spat the witch. 'We are surprised, but we forgive you, because that is the kind of big-hearted tyrants we are!'

'Speak for yourself, mother,' said Alvin between gritted teeth. 'I'm going to kill her, and then I'm going to run her over in my chariot, and then I'm going to feed the little pieces of her to my favourite snake...'

'I'M DEALING WITH THIS, ALVIN!' screeched the witch. 'But let me tell you, this mutiny changes nothing, Valhallarama, nothing! Your son, Hiccup, a *King*?'

Excellinor let out a high derisive cackle.

'How can you insult the dignity of this crowd by even suggesting such a thing! Are we to be ruled by slaves now? Your son Hiccup is a *slave*,' ground out the witch. 'And there is nothing you can do to change this, Valhallarama. Great Hero though you are, you cannot make the moving hand of time tick backwards. None of us can do that. The Slavemark is a Mark that no one can remove!'

Again, Valhallarama did not speak.

She had backed away from the witch towards Gumboil, who was holding a large basket full of weaponry and equipment.

Valhallarama took something long and thin from that basket.

Something long and thin that ended in a metal 'Ssss' glowing bright and dark. She held it up so that all could see clearly what it was.

The Vikings watched open-mouthed as Valhallarama the Hero took the brand in her hand, and placed it on her own forehead.

The Great Hero did not even flinch. And there, on her white forehead, bright and dark, was the glowing Mark.

Unthinkable! Impossible!

Valhallarama had put the Mark upon her own forehead!

She had turned the laws of the Archipelago upside-down and put the Mark on her own forehead.

29. AN UNEXPECTED DEVELOPMENT

Outside, the Dragon Rebellion roared, but inside, the courtyard was spellbound with quietness.

The witch was, quite simply, flabbergasted. She staggered back on her throne.

'What are you doing?' stammered the witch, thoroughly confused. 'You have turned yourself into a slave! What does this mean?'

'A Mark is just a symbol, witch,' said Valhallarama. 'And symbols can change. This is no longer the Slavemark, but the Dragonmark. I take this Mark as a sign of my love and my faith in my husband and my son.

I CALL UPON ALL THOSE WHO WOULD HAVE HICCUP AS THEIR KING TO TAKE THE DRAGONMARK WITH ME!

AND I CALL UPON ALL THOSE WHO WOULD
HAVE HICCUP AS THEIR KING TO TAKE THE
DRAGONMARK WITH ME!'

'So you have the situation under control do you,
Mother?' spat Alvin, savagely. 'Is this your idea of
control?'

'It's preposterous…' spluttered the witch.
'Ridiculous… The Slavemark is the Slavemark. It's
been like that for hundreds of years. What do you
mean, the *Dragonmark?* You can't just change things
like that. THERE'S NO SUCH THING AS A
DRAGONMARK! Valhallarama just made it up!'

Hiccup could not quite believe what was happening.

He looked around at the free Vikings' faces. Some of them were looking at the Silver Phantom. Others were looking at the floor. It was impossible to tell what they were thinking.

Valhallarama was taking a huge gamble.

It was asking way too much for someone to voluntarily take on a Mark that had been considered the ultimate in shame for as long as they could remember, to put at risk his Viking honour, out of mere concern for the fate of non-entities such as slaves and dragons. Who would do such a thing, especially for someone like Hiccup?

'You see?' sneered the witch, regaining her composure, as she realised no one was stepping forward.

'Nobody wants your so-called *Dragonmark*, or your runty little son as a leader, Valhallarama...'

Well, that's a good reason why Valhallarama should have hung on to the Dragon Jewel and nominated herself as the true King, thought Hiccup. *She's the kind of person that people will follow into battle, the kind of person people will lay down their lives for.*

But Hiccup had never been able to get anyone to come on to his team for Bashyball, let alone been the kind of person people risked their lives and honour for...

'*I* will take your Dragonmark!' came a ringing cry from the back.

Thuggory the Meathead strode forward, all six foot three of him.

Thuggory was the Heir to Mogadon the Meathead.

He was about sixteen years old, a huge hulking adolescent, who was thoroughly admired across the Archipelago as the very pattern of what a young Viking Hero ought to be. Many a Viking Chieftain had wished their own sons could be a little more like Thuggory.

Now his father Mogadon thundered out, 'Thuggory! I am ordering you as your father and your Chieftain! Do not dare take that Mark!'

But Thuggory strode forward nonetheless.

The crowd stood back to let him pass.

'I am sorry, Father,' cried Thuggory solemnly, and he bowed formally to his father as a son should. 'But Hiccup is right. If the dragons were free, they would not make war on us. It is time for a new world, a better one.'

Thuggory stopped in front of Valhallarama, very brisk and soldier-like, and knelt and removed his helmet as if he were becoming a Warrior.

Valhallarama put the Dragonmark on his forehead.

'Hiccup for King!' yelled Thuggory, jumping to his feet and punching the air.

'Well, only one person!' scoffed the witch. 'You're not going to get very far with only one foll—'

'Hiccup for King!' roared a whole cohort of young Meatheads, clearly friends of Thuggory.

Suddenly all around the courtyard, the young teenagers of the Tribes pressed forward to get the Mark. Camicazi landed in the courtyard with Fishlegs on the back of the Deadly Shadow, and had to push her way to the front and threaten several Danger-Brutes to get her Dragonmark first.

Because even the young of the conventionally

vicious Tribes such as the Danger-Brutes and the
Visithugs were clamouring for the Mark now.

How was this possible?

Well, a strange thing had happened during the
year of Hiccup being an Outcast.

Hiccup had turned from the most unlikely,
scrawny, puny little Viking ever, into a romantic figure
of rebellion.

Many of the younger Vikings had been secretly
following his progress as Hiccup set free dragon-traps
and eluded the forces of the Wilderwest in yet another
brilliant and hair-raising escape.

They had been whispering in secret stories
of Hiccup's adventures, and suddenly they were
whispering them not as evidence of what a weirdo he
was, how bizarre, how freakish, but of how clever, how
extraordinary, how bravely unusual he was...

'Have you heard how he discovered the Land
That Does Not Exist?' they had been whispering.

'Have you heard how he defeated the Sea
Dragon? The Strangulator? How he tricked the
Romans at the Fortress of Sinister? How he stopped
the Exterminators at Lava-Lout island? How he
slipped through the witch's fingers once again in the
land of Nowhere? How he found EVERY SINGLE

ONE of Grimbeard the Ghastly's Lost Things, and Alvin only stole them from him?'

When you put it like that, it seems extraordinary that no one had noticed what a Hero they had in their midst already. Short of going round with a big fat arrow on his head saying 'HERE IS THE GREATEST HERO YOU'VE HAD IN THE ARCHIPELAGO FOR CENTURIES' there isn't much more that Hiccup could have done to make this blindingly obvious.

But it can sometimes take a while for people to change their minds about things.

Even Hiccup's ridiculous birthday, the 29th of February of a Leap Year, a source of shame to him for his entire life, was suddenly in his favour.

'And I've heard he's only three years old,' they whispered, in hushed respect.

'To have done all this when he is only THREE YEARS OLD. Why it's superhuman!'

This is the way that legends begin.

You remember what I said, way way way back at the start of Hiccup's adventures, how this would be the story of becoming a Hero the Hard Way?

Now you can begin to see exactly how hard the way has been.

Alone, Hiccup had stood up against Alvin the Treacherous and the entire weight of the Tribes. Alone, he had stood up for what he believed in, for what he felt was right, even when everyone else thought he was wrong.

That was something, in the end, that the Vikings could respect.

And somehow, along the way, Hiccup with his masked dragonskin fire-suit, his inventive equipment, his raggedy Windwalker dragon, his championing of the weak and friendless, his weird little toothless hunting-dragon, his actually really-rather-cool tattoo...

(For when you come to think about it, a tattoo in the shape of a dragon on your forehead, is kind of cool.)

Somehow with all these things, Hiccup had become...

... a Hero.

And not just any old Hero either.

The sort of person people will follow into battle and risk their lives for.

A King.

It wasn't just the young either.

Even Mogadon the Meathead found himself looking anew at Hiccup, and changing his mind.

How is it that things can change so quickly, as it seems, in an instant?

The fact is that things had been changing anyway, without the Vikings really realising. The existence of Prison Darkheart had been an unspoken source of shame that the non-slave-trading Tribes had tried very hard to forget about.

Most of the Vikings were fond of the dragons they had grown up with, and even with the war going on, the thought of a world without dragons was depressing and frightening.

Plus the witch and Alvin had already enslaved many friends and relations, and a large number of people in that courtyard had a vague anxiety that they could be next.

So people had been changing their minds without really realising, and when things build to a tipping point, a revolution can happen in just five minutes.

'M-U-U-U-U-U-UTINYYYYYYYYY!!!!' screamed Alvin the Treacherous. 'LOYAL CITIZENS OF THE WILDERWEST, ARREST THESE TRAITORS, BURY THEM IN THE DEEPEST DARKEST DUNGEON YOU CAN FIND, AND THROW AWAY THE KEY!'

Absolute chaos then ensued in that Prison Darkheart, as in one life-changing second, everybody tried to decide which side they were on and, furthermore, work out which side everybody else was on, which wasn't so very easy on the spur of the moment like that.

All the slaves were on Hiccup's side of course, and some of the guards began to set them free from their chains immediately. Most Tribes like the Bog-Burglars, Peaceables and Hooligans were already thoroughly fed up with the whole Treacherous regime.

But the witch and Alvin still had plenty of supporters among the Murderous and Uglithug Tribes, the Danger-Brutes and the Berserks. I'm afraid there were plenty of vicious and heartless humans in that lot.

And because there wasn't time for everybody who wanted it to get themselves clearly marked with the Dragonmark so that everyone knew where they were, the ensuing battle very quickly became extremely confusing.

The night air rang with the bright sound of sword on sword, and cries of 'What are you doing? I'm on *your* side!' and 'Oh, I'm so sorry, I just assumed because you were a Murderous that you'd be for the witch,' and 'Oh, you did, did you? Well, let me tell you, some of us Murderous are just as sensitive as the next guy…' And so on.

Firing arrows at a ridiculously systematic rate, Valhallarama fought her way to Stoick's side and HIYYYAAHHH!!!! with one swing of her battle-axe she chopped through the chains that bound him.

Hiccup was close enough to hear what his mother said to Stoick.

'You were not my first love, Stoick the Vast,' said Valhallarama. 'But you are my last…'

Stoick's tired eyes lit up. And then Valhallarama grinned, just like she must have grinned, once, when she was a wild little girl.

'Welcome to the Company of the Dragonmark, Chief.' And she handed Stoick her second best sword.

Stoick's chest swelled. The years fell off him. For Thor's sake, he was not an old man after all, a little past his prime perhaps, but the best years of his life were ahead of him and he could feel the dance of war beginning to tingle in his feet...

'Valhallarama, my darling,' said Stoick, 'that is a lovely thing to say, and you were magnificent, as ever!'

Valhallarama had drawn the Nevermiss, and the two of them rang their two swords together grandly, affectionately, as if they were lifting glasses in a toast.

Roaring like a charging bull, Stoick launched back into battle, swinging his sword at Alvin's warriors, creaking a tiny bit at the knees perhaps, but mostly like he'd never really left.

'GUARDS OF THE WILDERWEST! COME FIGHT FOR YOUR KING!' screamed Alvin.

'NO!' yelled the witch. 'The Dragon Rebellion! Don't forget the Dragon Rebellion!'

But the guards on the battlements left their positions on Alvin's orders, and the attack of the Dragon Rebels became louder and more furious, and there was a danger that at any second now they would break through and overwhelm the prison itself.

30. THE BATTLE OF PRISON DARKHEART

No wonder they called this bay the Dragons' Graveyard. Indescribably sinister it was, this past and present battlefield, and the wind wailing through those dead dragon skeletons seemed to carry voices of a millennium of ghosts.

Now the tide had risen again and the living dragons were waking.

The red sand below the sea was giving birth to live dragons, swarming in their thousands out of the scarlet sand below and bursting out of the bay, and none of them were Hiccup's favourite species.

Serpent-tongues writhed and twisted around the white dragon bones, shaking out their wet wings. Sandrazors, Hellsteethers, Darkbreathers and Tonguetwisters joining them from the Forgotten Forest and the Open Ocean. The darkest types of dragon species, the monsters, the ones that hated the humans most.

They were chanting the beginning of the Red-Rage and sharpening their talons on the bones of their dead dragon brothers. They saw the little human ants and their terrible weapons of exploding fire and spears departing from the battlements, and they knew their time had come.

'MAKE RED your claws
with HUMAN BLOOD...
OBLITERATE the HUMAN FILTH...
Torch the humans like a WOOD
The ReBEllion is coming...'

Crouching in the centre of the ghastly graveyard of dragons' hopes and dreams and lives, was the Dragon Furious. It is difficult to describe the beauty of Furious. Now that he was no longer a captive, his skin, though scarred, had returned to its former glory. It was a blue so blue that you have never seen that colour before. Deeper than the blue sky, more royal than cerise, brighter than sapphires.

'The humans are fighting among themselves,' whispered Furious, and his eyes blazed with triumph.

And I mean, quite literally, blazed. An extraordinary feature of fully grown Sea Dragons is

that their eyes
can catch fire and
smoke. Little bursts of
bright red flame, as sharp as lasers,
darted from the pupils.

'ATTA-A-A-A-A-A-CCCKKKKKKK!!!!!!!'
roared the Dragon Furious to his second-in-command,
a great Sea Dragon called the Thunderer.

'ATTACK!'

And so

began the Battle for

Prison Darkheart.

For the first time in a thousand

years, the dragons of the Dragon Rebellion

flew over the undefended battlements, and into the

prison itself.

The humans fighting each other were now in

disarray. They could not reach their Exploding Things.

Their weapons of destruction were now being blown up by the magnificent winged serpents invading from above.

Valhallarama, under attack from warriors of the Wilderwest and dragons simultaneously, killed four Sandrazors that were launching themselves with sword sharp wings pointed straight at her neck, and shouted, 'COMPANIONS OF THE DRAGONMARK! RETREAT FROM THE PRISON AND MAKE FOR THE SHIPS! OUR STRONGHOLD SHALL BE THE BOG-BURGLAR ISLANDS TO THE WEST!'

Alvin and his supporters were now fleeing to the ships as well, and the witch was organising their own retreat to the Uglithug territories in the east.

Everyone had to make their choice. West for Hiccup and the Dragonmark, east for Alvin and the witch.

The Wodensfang and Toothless couldn't really choose of course, they were going with Alvin whether they liked it or not, for they were swinging in the amber-nets over Alvin's shoulder.

'We're going the wrong w-w-way!' squealed Toothless. 'We need to go with H-H-Hiccup! This is a disaster! Toothless is the most important Lost Thing, Hiccup can't possibly do without me!'

The Hairy Scary Librarian seemed to feel that maybe he was quits with Hiccup, and he had a new score to settle now that he had realised the emptiness of a witch's promise. So *he* headed west, to the Bog-Burglar Islands.

In the middle of the battle, Gobber the Belch passed Snotlout, deep in thought, looking to west and east.

Snotlout couldn't decide which way to go.

West
for
Hiccup
and the
Dragonmark

East

for
Alvin
and
the
Witch

Which way would
Snotlout Go?

He knew what the witch and Alvin were now, and he hated them almost as much as they scared him. But taking Hiccup as his King? His despised little runt-boy cousin? His pride revolted at the thought. Hiccup had stepped in to save Snotlout, but even *that* was kind of irritating.

'Snotlout!' called Gobber. 'You can still fight for the right side, Snotlout. You are one of the best Warriors I have ever taught. You remember the Black Star you won against Alvin at the Battle of the Lucky Thirteen? You'd be a tremendous asset to the Company of the Dragonmark. Come with us!'

Snotlout did not answer, and Gobber shrugged his shoulders, and left him there.

Snotlout reached into his pocket and took out the Black Star medal, one of the highest awards for bravery the Archipelago can bestow. He turned it over and over, trying to decide. West or east? West or east?

Which way would Snotlout go?

And that is where we will leave him, standing undecided in the middle of the battlefield.

Thinking.

Valhallarama fought her way across to Hiccup.

'DUCK!' yelled Valhallarama.

'What?'

'DUCK!' she yelled again, pushing him downwards, and firing an arrow over his head that killed a swooping Sandrazor stone dead mid-swoop.

'OK, Hiccup,' said Valhallarama. 'It is too dangerous for you to stay with us. Take the Jewel and hide from both dragon and Viking. Deadly Shadow dragons know how to hide. Make your way to Tomorrow for the Crowning day, and your father, the Company of the Dragonmark and I will meet you there. In the meantime, no one must know you are alive.'

'But I haven't got any of the Things!' protested Hiccup. 'Alvin has everything apart from the Jewel!'

'The Jewel is the most important Thing of all,' said Valhallarama. 'Be careful of it.'

Just before the Great Warrior turned away, back to the battle, Hiccup put his hand on his mother's metal arm. Even though he was particularly bedraggled after his long and tiring day, streaked with Monster juices and ocean, he was somehow *less* small and unlikely than he had ever been before.

He looked... Oh dear, what did he look like?

It was all such a long time ago.

But I think he looked a little more...

... grown-up.

'Thank you,' said Hiccup to Valhallarama.

'You have nothing to thank me for,' said Valhallarama. 'I am your mother. Oh and Hiccup...'

'Yes, Mother?'

'Don't be too hard on yourself, Hiccup,' said Valhallarama, and perhaps her smile was slightly sad now, 'if things do not turn out well in the end. I have learnt the hard way that Heroes can only do their best...'

Hiccup climbed on to the Deadly Shadow dragon. 'Camicazi! Fishlegs! COME ON!' he shouted down.

'Are we coming too?' asked Camicazi.

'Of course you're coming,' said Hiccup. 'I can't be an Outcast on my own again. Besides, the Deadly Shadow isn't mine, it belongs to Fishlegs.'

← the Throne

← the Crown

the heart's stone

the shield

the sword ↓

the...

There was one more thing to do.

Hiccup steered the Deadly Shadow above the head of King Alvin, fleeing as fast as he could, step TAP, step TAP, step TAP, through the battlefield towards the fleet.

Over Alvin's shoulder, bump bump bump, he carried the long poles of the Librarian's Heart-Slicers holding the two little dragons, the Wodensfang and Toothless, who were peering out, terrified, from the nets.

The Deadly Shadow hovered, perfectly camouflaged, above.

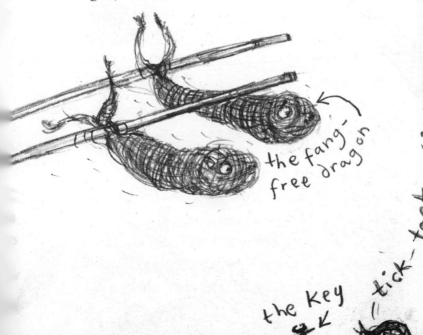

the fang-free dragon

the key

tick-tock, tick-tock, tick-tock, tick-tock, tick-tock, tick-tock

the ticking-thing

Hiccup
leant down
from the back
of the Deadly
Shadow and cut
the nets so that
the Wodensfang
and Toothless
flew free,
shooting
joyfully upwards,
Toothless
trumpeting
his rooster-crow of
triumph.

And in the very same moment,
Alvin looked up, clawed automatically
with his hook, and caught the chain of the
Jewel, swinging from Hiccup's neck.

'Shoot him!' screamed Alvin to his
Warriors. The camouflaged Deadly Shadow rose
up in a rain of arrows, the chain on Hiccup's
neck broke…

Toothless and the Wodensfang and the Deadly Shadow rose up to the battlements, arrows pouring upward after them... and...

'GOT IT!' shrieked Alvin, catching the Jewel in his other hand.

So after all that searching, all that drama, all the gazillions of words of this Quest, let's face it, the Jewel ended up in Alvin's horrible hooky hands after all.

Annoying, huh? Just one second, one false move on the part of the Hero, one lapse of concentration, that's all it takes, for everything to fall apart.

'NOOOOOO!!!' shouted Hiccup.

It was a scary sight to see the witch's face, as she saw the warm golden splendour of the Dragon Jewel dropping into the hook of her darling boy at last.

OH DEAR.

Alvin the Treacherous gets the Jewel...

The witch Excellinor let out a high, exultant cackle, and there, in the middle of the death and destruction of that battle she spread wide her bat-wing arms in jubilant conquest.

'I knew my predictions could not be wrong!' screamed the witch. 'I knew I had to be this brilliant for a reason! Thank you, O powers of death and darkness in whom I put my trust! Thank you, O fortunes most foul and most glorious! See!' she screeched, shaking her bony fist up at the heavens, 'see how we triumph!

'Let me see it, Alvin, my darling, let me have it.'

It was piteous to see the fragile amber beauty of that Jewel, glowing from within as if it were fire, cradled in the vile crooked hands of that fiend the witch.

She kissed it with her dry lips… crooned over it with a wicked whisper… and here is what she hissed as she held it in her hands at last:

'Watch out,' whispered the witch. 'Watch out, small innocent things growing in the sunshine… Watch out you splendid dragons with your giant spreading wings… for we can bring you down now, you who think you are so mighty… we can tear you from the sky and watch you *shrivel* in the mud…'

She grinned and that grin was truly terrifying.

'Watch out, dragons,' whispered the witch softly, 'for the dragons' days are numbered now… Watch out… watch out… watch out…'

She handed the precious Jewel back to her repulsive son, Alvin the Treacherous, and he put it carefully away in his armoured breast pocket.

So Hiccup had *found* the Dragon Jewel all right, but it had not stayed with him very long.

Alvin had the Jewel now and, step TAP, step TAP, step TAP, step TAP, he hurried to the east, his mother bounding after him on all fours, like a wolf-skeleton come to life, and the ticking-thing swinging from Alvin's waist ticking out a new and twisted tune.

Ti-i-i-ick-to-ock… ti-i-i-ick… to-o-o-ick… ti-i-i-i-ick… to-ii-ick…

Toothless was happy though, all unknowing as he was, of the malevolent intent of the witch and her horrible son.

The little dragon was just delighted to be reunited with his master once again.

'Cock-a-doodle-doo!' crowed Toothless.

'Don't worry, H-h-hiccup! Don't p-p-panic, everybody, Toothless is here! The most important Thing of all!'

Toothless, the Wodensfang and the Shadow rose up to the battlements of Darkheart as the great doors opened and the humans poured out to make their escape below.

Above their heads, for the first time in a thousand years, the dragons took Darkheart.

The Dragon Rebellion poured through the corridors of the Prison. There were Tonguetwisters in the courtyard setting fire to the long tables. They tore down the towers, sending them tumbling and crashing into the dungeons where their dragon ancestors had been kept in chains for centuries.

In the bay of the Dragons' Graveyard, the Dragon Furious crouched amid the chaos, his eyes scanning the skies above relentlessly in great searchlight beams, ignoring the Viking ships with their burning sails slaloming through the dragon skeletons all around him, sending out their Exploding Things as they shot their way out in retreat.

'The boy...' hissed the Dragon Furious. 'Where is the boy called Hiccup?'

The Dragon Furious was right, of course; the boy was there, soaring invisibly above the great dragon's head on the back of the Deadly Shadow.

For one second, the Dragon Furious saw him. A burst of Exploding Thing Fire must have caught the Shadow off-guard. For one moment he turned visible with the shock, and there he was, with Hiccup on his back, right in the Dragon Furious's searchlight eyebeams.

The Dragon Furious saw the Deadly Shadow… he was sure he saw it… and gave a cry of astonished rage.

The dragon that he had sent to kill Hiccup, the dragon who claimed he hated humans as strong as acid, had turned his allegiance and was now *helping* the boy!

How could this be? He had chosen this dragon most particularly for his hatred of human beings...

He had chosen this dragon particularly because he was so like the Dragon Furious himself...

But there was Hiccup, clearly outlined on the back of the Shadow, Camicazi and Fishlegs beside him, three little hunting-dragons hovering above like flies, and the three heads of Innocence, Arrogance and Patience sending out lightning bolts in three different directions.

How did the boy do it?

What was it about him?

The Dragon Furious spread wide his great blue wings, and made a final despairing leap.

One second the Hiccup-boy on the back of the dragon was there. The next the dragon turned the exact stormy grey of the sky.

Dragon, boy and companions simply disappeared, as the now-invisible Deadly Shadow streaked across the sky.

Dragon Furious's great jaws closed on nothing. His gigantic claws tore only on the air.

He crashed back down into the Dragons' Graveyard, boy-less, and in despair.

The Dragon Furious howled, and plunged through the bay, flinging great boulders around, uprooting any living vegetation he could find, tearing up the airy grasses on the islands that contained no boy, his own Tonguetwisters and Rageblasts of the Rebellion whimpering like terriers, and trying to stay out of the way.

Finally, in one screaming blast of white-hot fire, the Dragon Furious incinerated the whole bay, annihilated it in the blaze of his defeated and baffled fury.

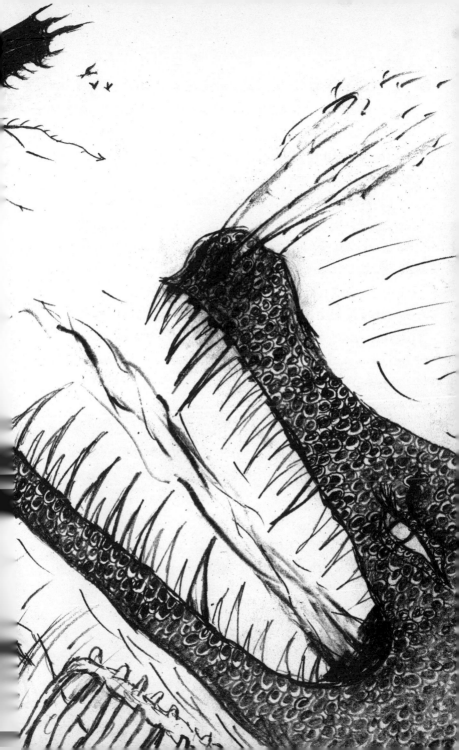

And then crouched down, panting, in
the middle of the blaze like a great blue cat, lying in
the centre of the great night-time graveyard of his
fellow dragons' bones. Fear was in the blazing eyes
now.

Gone...

The boy was gone.

As the Dragon Furious's rage died down, he
seemed to shrink in front of your eyes.

That brilliant blue faded from his skin, and
became a more ordinary shade. He even curled up
into a defensive ball, like an ordinary fireside cat,
hiding his head in his dragon hands, as if he did

not want to use his own power of looking into the Future.

A human with a heart might have felt sorry for the great creature, leaning his poor scarred head on the blazing fire of his own making like it were a pillow.

'One more chance gone,' the dragon whispered, hissing to himself. 'Surely we cannot be facing extinction?

'Surely that cannot be the dragons' fate at last?'

A great Sea Dragon, a Thunderer, came joyfully to tell the news to Furious.

'The day is won, Furious! Darkheart is fallen!'

It was a glorious moment for the dragons.

The Vikings had escaped – *just*.

The Vikings were lucky that any of them made it through the white hot fury of the Dragon Rebellion assault that day.

Only by valiant fighting, with the utmost skill of sword and shield and spear did the Viking fleets escape, shooting and blasting their way through the numberless talons and teeth, the scorching devastation of the dragons' flames.

Even then, it was with bloodied burning boats, sails on fire, and many of their numbers lost.

The Company of the Dragonmark made their way to the Bog-Burglar Islands, and the witch and her Warriors to the Uglithug lands in the east.

But the dragons had Darkheart at last.

So the Thunderer was surprised to find Furious in such abject misery.

'Furious... What is wrong? Surely this is our finest hour?'

'You do not understand,' growled Furious. 'The boy Hiccup has escaped.'

'But one human boy,' said the Thunderer in surprise. 'Surely one little human boy, so small, so pink, no talons, no fire... Surely one little boy cannot matter so very much?'

'This is no ordinary boy,' replied Furious.

And then, he uncurled himself and rose up, slowly, dangerously, like a phoenix from the ashes.

His body began to burn bright again.

'He must never grow up,' vowed the Dragon Furious. 'He must never reach the island of Tomorrow.

'Never again shall I make the mistake of entrusting his killing to someone else,' panted the Dragon Furious. 'This time I will kill him myself... I shall seek him everywhere. I shall tear the world apart looking for him. Nowhere shall be safe for him: no cave, no cliff, no rock, no island. I shall turn this whole world to ashes, looking for him.

'Hear the pledge of the Dragon Furious!' screamed the dragon, his whole body screeching with fury, so much so that even his eyeballs began to smoke and pour out flame, and then he bent his head backwards, sending fire upwards with the scream, like an erupting volcano.

'THE BOY SHALL NEVER REACH TOMORROW!'

31. THE SECRET HIDEOUT

Somewhere not very far away (I don't want to tell you
exactly where, because it is Hiccup's secret hideout,
and it really, really needs to be kept a secret) the
Windwalker was lying in front of a cave surrounded by
brambles.

He had been lying there, protecting the entrance,
for nearly three days now, and he was a bedraggled,
wet sight, his ears drooping sadly, his spines all limp
and floppy with loneliness as he listened to the sound
of the Dragon Furious's rage.

And then...

He sniffed the air, he peered upwards...

... his ears pricked up in sudden apprehension.

And so too would yours if a semi-visible cloud

descended down out of nowhere, and slowly turned into a terrifying-looking, heavily armed, three-headed Deadly Shadow dragon.

However Hiccup peered over the side of the Deadly Shadow's wings and shouted down: 'Don't worry, Windwalker, it's only us!'

The Windwalker sprang to greet the horror of the Deadly Shadow descending towards him, flying round and round and round it, in wild excited joy.

So late that night, the little cave whose whereabouts shall remain a secret, was very full indeed, for even when the Shadow camouflaged himself so well he looked invisible, he didn't get any smaller. He was a very large dragon, and once he was inside the cave, there was barely room for everyone else.

The Windwalker had gone out every single day and caught plenty of fish, in the hope that they would return. So that was a joyful and triumphant evening, with everyone back together again recalling the triumphs and successes of the day.

'Y-y-yes, Stormfly,' sang Toothless happily. 'Wodensfang the Desperado and I sh-sh-shot our way out of those amber-nets. Peow! Peow! Peow! with three bursts of our super-strong flame and...'

And so on.

Meanwhile, Stormfly flashed her wicked eyes at him and ate half his mackerel.

'*Manners*,' sniffed the Wodensfang disapprovingly.

The ten companions stuffed themselves full with fish that night, ate until they could eat no more. What with the food, and the emotion of the day, Hiccup and the others were almost drunk with happiness, in fits of laughter about the smallest things.

In times of war and deadly peril, these moments of happiness are heightened: they become even more pleasurable, even more precious.

Hiccup was one of the last to fall asleep.

But then he woke again, at the sound of the Dragon Furious demolishing Prison Darkheart and turning it to rubble. That woke him, and suddenly all the warmth and the happiness of the evening seemed to disappear, to be replaced by a cold dread and a thumping of his heart.

The others were all so exhausted, they were

The ten Companions of the Dragonmark

still fast asleep.

But blink, blink, the twin eyes of the Wodensfang opened on Hiccup's chest, and the eyebeams shone comfortably into Hiccup's own eyes.

The Wodensfang seem to guess immediately what Hiccup was thinking.

He started chatting, to cheer Hiccup up.

'You see,' said the Wodensfang. 'I told you your Quest was quite simple. See what can be achieved if your heart is in your Quest? You have found your friend... You have found the Jewel... um... Even though it has fallen into Alvin's hands for the moment, I am sure that it will come back to you again...'

(The Wodensfang tried to sound more sure of this than he was actually feeling.)

'And you are no longer so alone. Look how full this cave is! You have your human companions, now,' he gestured with his wing to Fishlegs and Camicazi, 'not to mention all the followers your splendid mother has brought you with her Dragonmark. What a magnificent warrior she is!' said the Wodensfang admiringly.

'Anyway,' said the Wodensfang, 'as I was saying, the rest of the Quest should be a piece of fish-cake. Now all the Lost Things are found, all you have to do is present yourself at the island of Tomorrow, get yourself crowned King instead of Alvin the Treacherous, learn the Secret of the Jewel, and use it to persuade the Dragon Furious to call off this war... See what I mean? Easy peasy, viking squeezy!'

Hiccup was not to be so easily comforted.

'You've forgotten a few important details,' Hiccup reminded him.

'I just heard the Dragon Furious and something tells me he's going to be impossible to persuade. And Alvin the Treacherous has *nine* of the Lost Things, which might make the Tomorrow Men think that Alvin is the true King. *I* only have one. And Alvin has the Dragon Jewel, and we know what kind of man Alvin is. He would use the Jewel's power to destroy the dragons, without even blinking.'

'Ah, but Alvin won't do anything with the Jewel... yet,' said the Wodensfang. 'Alvin needs that Jewel to take to Tomorrow if he wants to become the King himself. And only if he became the King would he learn the Jewel's secret. We are perfectly safe... for the moment, admittedly.'

Hiccup sat up on his bed of grass, filled with

sudden, desperate anxiety.

He looked straight into the Wodensfang's brown eyes earnestly. 'Doesn't it worry you, Wodensfang, that I only had the Dragon Jewel for a few minutes before it fell into the hands of Alvin the Treacherous?'

The Wodensfang said nothing.

'I've just been worrying and worrying about it. Do you remember the last time you trusted a human with the Dragon Jewel? Hiccup the First? And how eventually it fell into the hands of Grimbeard the Ghastly? What if this is history repeating itself? It does seem that I collect all these Things, but they all end up in the hands of Alvin the Treacherous...

'Maybe you shouldn't be trusting me, Wodensfang,' said Hiccup. 'What if the Dragon Furious is right? He told me that I would be the one who sent the dragons into their final oblivion... Maybe that's because I'm going to collect all the Lost Things, and then Alvin is going to use them to destroy the dragons.'

Hiccup covered his face in horror.

'I can't bear to think of it – but that is what the Deadly Shadow said, that Alvin could not get hold of the Jewel without me finding it for him. If that is true, then is it all going to be my fault?'

It was a truly dreadful thought. A world without dragons. A world with no Windwalker. No more flying on his back. No more soaring into the clouds in slow beats of the Windwalker's wings, up, up, up and looking down on the islands of the Archipelago sprinkled way, way down below.

A world without Toothless, perching on your arm, giving you that naughty look, opening up his greengage eyes so innocently as he tells you that he's going to do something you wanted him to do, he p-p-promises, cross his claws and hope to die, and then flies off and does precisely what he wants?

No, it was too horrible to think about. And all to be Hiccup's fault?

No, and again no. Never, never, never.

But then again, things can go awry, even if you have the best of intentions...

'Nonsense and fiddlesticks,' replied the Wodensfang. 'You are young. Leave these worries to us old creatures. I trust you, Hiccup. Besides, don't forget, Alvin the Treacherous doesn't have ALL the Lost Things... You still have one of them, one that you have always been able to hang on to.'

He pointed with his wing at Toothless.

Toothless was fast asleep, curled up reassuringly warm and solid and heavy and alive on Hiccup's tummy, and snoring great grey smoke rings. So he made them both jump when he said loudly and clearly in his sleep: 'Yes, *I'm a Lost Thing*... *and I'm the most important one of all*... *Thank you*... *Manners*...'

That made both Hiccup and the Wodensfang laugh, and Hiccup fell asleep at last.

But it was the Wodensfang who could not sleep now.

Eventually he flew to the entrance of the cave, and curled into a little wrinkled ball, looking up at the night sky.

'*I have to confess*,' said the Wodensfang to the stars, '*this is worrying me a trifle, too. What can I do to prevent this from happening? Am I right in trusting the boy?*'

It didn't seem possible that a world without dragons could ever exist. Look at the world, filled with dragons everywhere, dragons of all shapes and sizes. The great ones, larger than the Big Blue Whale, half-swimming, half-flying through the oceans. The tiny little nanodragons hopping through the heather in their numberless multitudes. The cliffs and their mazy rocks beneath just teeming, bursting, *overflowing* with the abundance of dragon life.

Such was the generosity of nature, and the multiplicity of dragon species, surely it could never happen?

The stars looked down on the Wodensfang, winking at him, just as they had done for thousands of years.

And of course the stars made no answer.

So the Wodensfang answered his own question.

'Perhaps I am a foolish, fond old dragon, who never learns from his own mistakes. But I have to believe that the humans and the dragons are capable of living together. I have to hope that the impossible can be possible. I have to trust in the boy, and hope for the best...'

I have to trust in the boy, and hope for the best.

I have to hope for the best.

EPILOGUE BY HICCUP HORRENDOUS HADDOCK III

Last night I did not sleep well. I am an old man, and I dreamt I went back to the Amber Slavelands, flying over those windy sands like I was the Deadly Shadow, following a set of footprints across the desert desolation.

At first I thought they were the footprints of the Monster.

And then I realised they were the footprints of my childhood self.

Eventually I caught up with him, a scarecrow of a boy, struggling defiantly across those dreadful sands. And in this dream a great wind had come up, and all around him the blackened, burning remains of Hiccup's past went bowling past – the houses of the Hooligan village where he grew up, the skeletons from the Dragons' Graveyard – all blown away by the winds of the war that Hiccup had begun.

But the boy still walked onwards, towards Tomorrow.

What was it my mother Valhallarama had said? 'Don't be too hard on yourself, Hiccup, if things do not turn out well in the end...'

I know what awaits Hiccup on Tomorrow, so in my dream I tried to shout to the boy-I-once-was, 'Go back! Do not go to Tomorrow! Stay where you are!'

But of course my boyhood self could not hear me.

'STOP!' I shouted in my dream, but how could he hear me above the roaring of the wind that was blowing away the world all around him?

And even if he could, it is already too late for him to go back. The winds of the Amber Slavelands have already blown in the Rebellion. They have torched the little Hooligan village where I grew up. No one could live in those black smoky ruins.

And even if he could hear me, would I really want him to do anything differently?

Would I really want the ticking-thing to stop, for time to stand still, for Hiccup never to grow up, or to be something other than the boy he is?

This is all his— sorry, *my* fault, but if Hiccup had not acted as he did, there would still be slaves in the Amber Slavelands, Eggingarde would never have made it back to the arms of Bear-mama, the Dragon Furious would still be in chains, the world would still be back in the terrible barbaric times of slaves and tyrants and witches, and monsters with no hearts.

You see, it was not only Hiccup who was growing up, it was the entire world around him – and when whole worlds grow up, that can be painful and difficult.

Was it all worth the Archipelago in flames?

I do not know, you decide.

But Hiccup could not be anything other than the boy he was, and so his footsteps do not stop; they walk on. With every step he is a little older than he was before, walking slowly towards me and into Tomorrow.

The chapter in my life that Hiccup has just walked through has been a story of three mothers: Valhallarama, Bear-mama and Termagant.

Of how even when they are not there, when we cannot see them, when they are parted from us by quests, or by slavery, or even by death itself, they are still watching over us, yearning for us, loving us, though they lurk in the clouds as invisible to our eyes as the Deadly Shadow.

Far away by cold campfires they are thinking of us, dreaming of us, loving us long-distance.

Fishlegs's mother could not come back to hold him. She had gone behind that glass wall of death. But still she held up her hand from behind the glass, and pressed it up to Fishlegs's hand and willed him to be alive, to walk, to laugh, to love. As if she could breathe life into him, as if she could be there with him, as if she could pass through the glass with the sheer hopeless longing of her love.

And perhaps she *was* still there to love him.

Termagant's eyes had once shone into the six eyes of the Deadly Shadow.

The reflection of those eyes now shone back into the eyes of Fishlegs, so it was almost as if, sometimes, she herself were looking back at him. When the Shadow dragon pressed itself protectively against Fishlegs, it was an echo of the embrace that Termagant had given that same Shadow dragon once, long ago.

The past never really leaves us.

And now I am an old, old man, I hover over my childhood self, as if I were a dead mother, and I am anxious for Hiccup's future, because I already know it, and I want to protect the boy from pain.

But I am happy too, because I know the future is a curious mixture of joy and sadness.

So suddenly I throw away my fear, and I no longer shout 'Stop!'

I am shouting something slightly different now.

Walk on, Hiccup!
Have courage!
Walk into Tomorrow...
And I will meet you there at Hero's End...

THE
BOY SHALL
NEVER
REACH
TOMORROW...

*Oh dear, now things are looking even worse than they were at the end of the last book, and the Dragon Furious has sworn to **KILL** Hiccup himself...*

What path will Snotlout take, will he follow the witch, or will he go with Hiccup?

*How will the Ten Companions of the Dragonmark stop Alvin, now that he has **NINE** of the King's Lost Things?*

They must all make their way to Tomorrow for the

FINAL CONFRONTATION...

Can Hiccup save the dragons from extinction???????

Watch out for the next volume of Hiccup's memoirs...

This is Cressida, age 9, writing on the island.

Cressida Cowell grew up in London and on a small, uninhabited island off the west coast of Scotland where she spent her time writing stories, fishing for things to eat, and exploring the island looking for dragons. She was convinced that there were dragons living on the island, and has been fascinated by them ever since.

www.cressidacowell.com

HOWDEEDOODEETHERE!

For your latest news on all things dragon
and Cressida Cowell please follow:

@cressidacowellauthor

@cressidacowell

facebook.com/
cressidacowellbooks

Toodleoon for now...

LOOK OUT FOR
CRESSIDA COWELL'S
NEW SERIES

This is the story of a young boy Wizard,
and a young girl Warrior, who have
been taught to hate each other like poison.

#wizardsofonce